PULP
Literature

PULP LITERATURE PRESS

Issue No. 45, Winter 2025

Publisher: Pulp Literature Press; Editor-in-Chief: Jennifer Landels; Acquisitions Editor: Mel Anastasiou; Senior Editor: Sierra Louie; Poetry Editors: Daniel Cowper & Emily Osborne; Copy Editor: Amanda Bidnall; Russian Editor: Anna Belkine; Proofreader: Sierra Louie; Graphic Design: Amanda Bidnall & Sierra Louie; Cover Design: Kate Landels; Subscriptions: Carol McCauley; Advertising: Jared Schellenberg; First Readers: Amber Allen, Mark Cameron, Michaela Chan, Summer Keown, Sylvia Leong, Tara Smalldon. For advertising rates, direct inquiries to info@pulpliterature.com.

Cover painting, *Solstice Ritual* by Herman Lau. Illustrations for 'Say Cheese, Jesus, Please' by Rina Piccolo. All other illustrations by Mel Anastasiou.

Pulp Literature: ISSN 2292-2164 (Print), ISSN 2292-2172 (Digital), Issue No. 45, Winter 2025.

Published quarterly by Pulp Literature Press, 21955 16 Ave, Langley, BC, Canada V2Z IK5, pulpliterature.com, at $18.00 per copy. Annual subscription $60.00 in Canada, $80.00 in continental USA, $92.00 elsewhere. Printed in Surrey, BC, Canada, by Fraser Printers Ltd. Copyright © 2025 Pulp Literature Press. All stories and works of art copyright © 2025 their authors as per bylines.

Pulp Literature Press is based in the unceded traditional Coast Salish Territories of the Katzie, Kwantlen, Matsqui, and Semiahmoo First Nations.

Pulp Literature Press gratefully acknowledges the support of the Canada Council for the Arts and the Government of Canada.

Pulp Literature is a proud member of the Magazine Association of BC and Magazines Canada.

TABLE OF CONTENTS

FROM THE PULP LIT PULPIT

"A wave of progress is rising and rising . . ."
~ Spirit of the West, 'Darkhouse'

Vancouver band Spirit of the West's album *Labour Day* came out in 1988, but the lyrics are surprisingly relevant today. From homelessness and substance use in 'Gottingen Street' and 'Drinking Man', a housing crisis in 'Profiteers', and trans- and homophobia in 'Take It from the Source', there's a familiarity in these topics. The earworm that keeps circling my brain most often these days is 'Darkhouse', a lament about the loss of lighthouse keepers to computerized systems. Lines like "Soon we'll be watching the world turn / with no hands at all" and "Burning the bridge between our rise and fall," seem like they could just as easily refer to our ever-more-automated world, including the rapid rise of machine learning, aka 'Artificial Intelligence'.

Here at Pulp Literature Press, we're fans of the past. After all, our name and format pays homage to the twentieth-century pulp mags that kindled a bonfire of creative genius in genre fiction. We publish in print because we believe a beautiful, physical book is a joy to read that gets passed from hand to appreciative human hand. And we believe in the written work of a human brain.

But we're not Luddites. We embrace the technology that allows us to create and distribute a magazine from our desktops, and are delighted to have digital subscribers who devour our weightless ebook editions. And while we honour the written words that have come before us, we strive to publish stories by new voices, from demographics less heard in the past, with fresh, genre-defying ideas.

These are the choices that all of us have to make in times of technological and societal upheaval: to cherish what we love from the past and choose with care which future to embrace. At Pulp Lit, we choose not to publish any works created in part or whole by machine learning tools. And we reject the patriarchal, racist, sexist, ableist, and homophobic tropes of the literary past. We seek new and better stories crafted by good old human intelligence.

With this issue we bid fond farewell to beloved Acquisitions Editor Genevieve Wynand, who is moving on to a somewhat louder career with a pair of sticks. In her place we welcome our youngest ever senior editor, card-carrying Gen-Zedder Sierra Louie. Sierra's graphics skills and keen proofing eye have already been making *Pulp Literature* cleaner and more beautiful over the past two years, and we're delighted to see her taking on a larger role in curating the stories you find in these pages. And we're confident that the addition of young blood at the senior editors' table will keep these salty dogs from being replaced by a 'chip in the sea'.

The new year is a chance to look both forward and back, to embrace revolution and evolution, while honouring the past. Pour yourself a cup of something warm, settle in for some transformative tales, and maybe put on some Spirit of the West as you read.

~ *Jennifer Landels*

In THIS ISSUE

Solstice Ritual by cover artist **Herman Lau** challenges us with a winter landscape where myth and folklore lurk.

Adopt a revolutionary spirit with feature author **George McWhirter**'s 'Grillo, the Story of a Cricket', and defy the oligarchs in 'Baba Yaga and the Bear' by **Gregg Chamberlain**.

Poet **Dan MacIsaac** takes us back to ancient Crete with 'Pholoe', while **DA Cooper** brings blessed sleep to Valhalla in 'Ragnabeðtími'.

In 'Their Grandfather's Chair' by **JM Landels**, Allaigna's sisters are forced out of their comfort zone and onto separate paths, while returning to childhood memories is prickly and uncomfortable in 'The Past as Foundation for the Family Home' by **Shelley Lavigne** and 'Say Cheese, Jesus, Please' by **Rina Piccolo**.

The writing muse strikes at inopportune times in 'How to Write a Novel in Ten Days During the Zombie Apocalypse' by **Jakob Drud** and 'Take My Hand: Enter Night' by **Mel Anastasiou**.

And flash fiction from Hummingbird Prize winners **Cheryl Skory Suma, Adam Fout**, and **Soramimi Hanarejima** offers a look at difficult relationships in their many incarnations.

GRILLO, THE STORY OF A CRICKET

George McWhirter

George McWhirter's most recent fiction has been featured in The Fiddlehead *and is scheduled to appear in an upcoming* SubTerrain. *He has been anthologized in* Cli-Fi: Canadian Tales of Climate Change *(Exile Editions, 2017), and Exile's* CVC: Carter V. Cooper Short Fiction Anthology Series, Book Three *and* Book Four. *Exile Editions also published a book of his short stories and a novella,* The Gift of Women, *in 2015. He writes and publishes poetry as well as translating the contemporary Mexican poets Homero Aridjis, José Emilio Pacheco, and Gabriel Zaid. His translation of Homero Aridjis'* Self-Portrait in the Zone of Silence *(New Directions, 2023) was awarded the 2024 Griffin Prize for Poetry. George McWhirter was the judge of our inaugural Magpie Award for Poetry in 2014, and you can find 'Stalk', his sci-fi take on Jack and the Beanstalk, in* Pulp Literature *Issue 9, Winter 2016.*

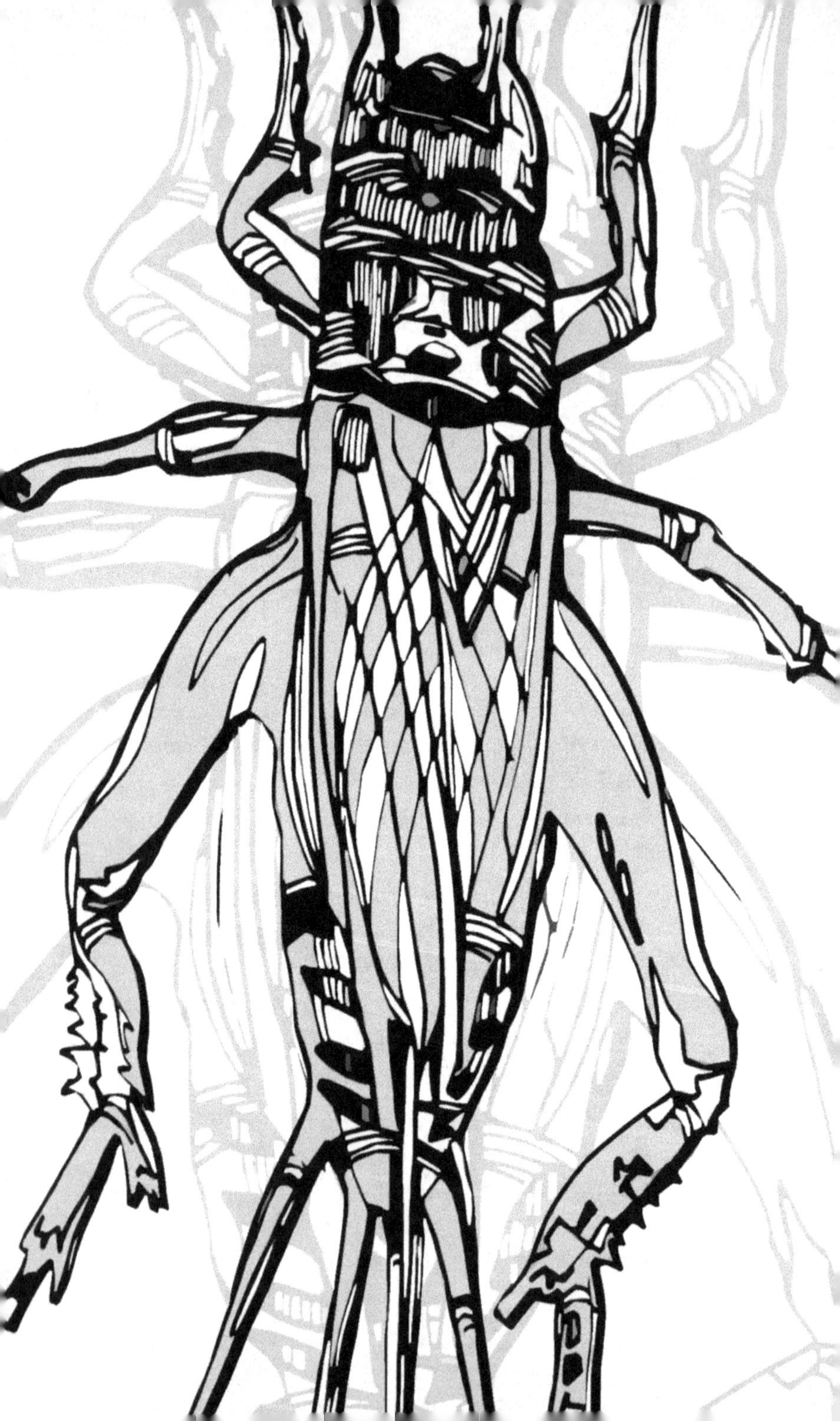

GRILLO, THE STORY OF A CRICKET

Cuautla, Morelos, 28 November 1990

A former co-researcher's study in *Perifèria* (University of Barcelona) on a Catalan *curandero* in Agrument has prompted my return to Cuautla, in Morelos, to resume research for my own article on a curandero who practises in Mexico. Even when I was a boy, the famous curandero's name was known to me from our visits to my mother's parents. They died in Cuautla within days of each other in 1975, and here I am, fifteen years later, ready to meet the renowned Martí and explore any Indigenous innovation he has introduced to the Catalan practice.

On a Friday in the third week of my visits to his home, I meet another visitor, Don Fausto Iribás, who is neither a patient nor one of Martí's associates. No sooner does Don Fausto learn that I am a trained clinical psychologist and anthropologist than he invites me to observe and answer a strange question about his sleep. That is, which insect most resembles his nocturnal behaviour when he lapses into a state beyond dream or anything like a normal sleep. Immediately, Martí takes pains to reassure me that the gentleman is a government minister and hacienda owner, a rational man of stature and responsibility. Also, we have something in common: both of us have studied for postgraduate degrees at Harvard. Surreal as it may seem (and highly unprofessional to indulge a delusion), I am nevertheless too curious to resist the visitor's claim to be a soulmate of Kafka's hero in 'The Metamorphosis'.

On an early morning tour of Don Fausto's estate my host demonstrates that his is a model hacienda, employing a manager and agricultural workers for the crops of avocado, banana, agave, and maguey crops. The agave's root-bowl is dug out, crushed, and distilled into tequila, while the maguey milk from the stem is fermented into pulque. The benefits of all production go to those who labour to produce it. My host traces the raison d'être for the organization of the hacienda to its source in his soul's extraordinary origins.

For me, the investigation into the identity of the insect and the nature of what he calls his soul starts with a follow-up breakfast meeting at his hacienda home. I begin with a question about the nocturnal vigil I will undertake.

You say I will be the first person ever to spend the night with you?

Yes. I have never spent the night with anyone, never wanted to, nor have I let anyone spend the night with me who wanted to, not since I was a boy. Even then, my brothers kicked me out of my separate bed and kept complaining until they forced me into a room of my own in this very house. As for me, being the eldest, some might say it's the way it should have been — and, sadly, needed to be. You see, when we were older and out of the nursery, my father wanted me and my brothers to share a room, as though we were little military cadets in a barracks. There is a cavalry barracks not far off, on the way from Cuautla to the Agua Hedionda spa. That may have given my father the idea.

But surely your brothers must have observed you as you slept. Why did you not ask them?

Yes, my brothers must have seen and heard me in the night. They could have confirmed or disabused me of my conviction, as my father might have or my mother, but I never dared tell or ask them as I am telling and asking you. My mother at first feared crib death and kept turning me onto my side, but no sooner would she leave the nursery than I would return to the same position she feared would kill me. My father's troop of three little Iribás soldiers served well when my brothers were small. With pony riding and playing, my brothers fell straight to the bottom of their dreams, like the stones they threw into the River Cuautla. But when they grew older and woke with erections, they believed, because I was older than them, that I had bigger and more troublesome erections. To which I responded with an ultra-religious sense of sin and engaged in contorted and punishing prayers, like those self-flagellating penitents during Easter week.

So your brothers and your mother did give you some information regarding your nocturnal behaviour?

My brothers were cruelly concise. To them I was 'un loco', 'un maniaco religioso'. But don't let me talk you out of eating your breakfast. Tuck into your chilaquiles, the poor man's chicken, and your refried beans, your hash browns, cooked especially for you with shredded potatoes, sausage, diced ham and bacon. I prepared it myself because I need something to do if I am not going directly into Mexico City to do my government business. Also, the first glimmer of light wakens me, and when I am here,

I come down into these kitchen quarters to cook breakfast. As I do for myself, I do for you this morning. Ceramically tiled caves, are they not? Like the Convent of Santa Clara's kitchens in Puebla, but without nuns, except for my mother in her time. She had them designed this way. My poor mother was turned into a solitary, religious soul by her long vigil over my nocturnal condition as I grew up. My poor, poor mother, all but abandoned by my father for his banking business in Mexico City. And my brothers, when they came of age, were regimented into the same business in the city, over one hundred kilometres away. However, the neurologists my mother brought in, quietly in the dead of night, diagnosed my condition (after one quick look through my bedroom door) as that of a nocturnal epileptic.

But you said no one had ever spent the night observing your condition.

I confess my mother did, but I never asked her or told her what I believed was going on in that place reserved for dreams or, more precisely in my case, visions. Better she believed me a nocturnal epileptic or *un maniaco religioso* acting out some endless penance rather than, God forbid, realizing that her son believed he existed as a cricket or a grasshopper in a previous life and that the nocturnal behaviours of his body derived from the insect's form and instinctive activity in that other life.

I comprehend your reticence. Telling your family you were a cricket or grasshopper in the night would be a shock to them and might subject you to endless psychiatric analysis at their request. I take it that I am not here with you for that purpose——an overnight assessment?

No, of course not. I just wish you to observe my physical behaviour. But eat your breakfast. I see your eyes going around the domes in the ceiling, around the curved blue tile with which my mother chose to cover them as if the domes are the firmaments of several heavens that one walks under when one comes in here to cook and eat. It is an effect she desired for herself every day, in the here and now: a blue heaven above and around her.

No need to turn to the right at the little white light and carry right on to my blue heaven?

Pardon?

Words of an old song. Fats Domino, 'My Blue Heaven'.

Very good, but after you have eaten, you may prefer to see the true, shining blue dome of the sky outside, without a cloud of steam off a pot of black beans drifting across it, filling your nostrils with fresh relish before you have even finished breakfast. I am not sure if you will enjoy what I am cooking for *la comida*, but no sooner did I set up breakfast for you than I moved on to assembling a pot of black beans which takes some time to slow-cook. Being my own chef allows me time to think. As is obvious.

From insect to human soul direct, you told me in our walk around the hacienda grounds. Was the 'insect to human soul direct' a teaser?

I knew it would pique your curiosity and perhaps commit you to collecting evidence of such a possibility from my side of the reincarnation conundrum. It represents the reverse of a normal order of regression from human to animal, fish, fowl, or insect in order to refine some crude elements of a soul that has not achieved true humility in its lifetime — or a proper appreciation of its privilege in being born human. But you know the problem I have posed for you.

Cricket or grasshopper: which of the two would you prefer?

I hope I am *la encarnación directa de un grillo*, which has never had a soul passed down through any previous incarnation as a human. I hope I am not the product of a male and female grasshopper copulating, with that ugly male mounting of the female that defines the grasshopper's crude coitus. I prefer to be the issue of mating crickets and a product of their more mysterious coupling, where the female enjoys the privilege of dominance and has this uncanny power to choose which sperm from which male she will use to fertilize her eggs. Her power to select her offspring makes her, to my mind, goddess-like. But after observing my sleeping behaviours, you will be in a position to confirm or dismiss my belief that I am the issue of a gloriously gravid cricket. My belief means that I am no random creature — that I was chosen and in turn was calling to be chosen by a female in my entomological existence before that moment of entering my crudessence as a human soul.

The moment of your crudessence — when exactly was that?

In the deepest hour of the night I remember the moment, and I remember exactly where it came to be. I leapt beyond the threshold of this very hacienda, the Chinameca Hacienda by the River Cuautla, where a great man fell in its doorway, and in my leaping and his falling, I landed in the coagulating blood of a bullet wound.

Was this something else you were afraid of telling?

Yes. And other things I did not dare disclose — other details of events before that moment.

What details?

Well, at that very moment when Zapata …

So the great man was Emiliano Zapata?

Yes, he died here, he came tumbling down without a chance to draw a pistol. I keep wondering if I was drawn to the warmth of the afternoon sun on the stone floor in the doorway, or if I headed for the doorway to dodge the boots of the Nationalist soldiers under Guajardo's command inside. Or was it the other way round — did I stray into that doorway from the fields?

Guajardo . . . Who was Guajardo?

Colonel Guajardo, Commander of the Fiftieth Regiment of Nationalist troops. Guajardo betrayed Zapata after vowing to join with him against *Presidente* Carranza. They met here at the Hacienda Chinameca to do just that — or so Zapata thought, but Guajardo had lured him into a trap. The moment of Zapata's death came in the afternoon. At that time of day, he was tricked by his hunger and an invitation from his murderer to come in to share tacos and beer. Alas, bullets were all that Emiliano tasted, which makes me wonder if my own fear or hunger at that moment made me leap.

What do you mean by that?

I mean, did I leap out of fear at the sound of gunshots, or out of hunger? Who knows what gunshots mean to a cricket or a grasshopper? On the other hand, hunger . . . a cricket's appetites are well-known. House crickets have as much a penchant as moths for clothing. In that moment, did I want to chew on what was laid out before me on the floor like a banquet — on Zapata's well-worn clothing? I know it sounds ridiculous when I try to reduce my responses to the primal set of an *acheta*. No matter; I know nothing of everything that went before, which is irrelevant in any case, for I ended up glued in blood to a bullet wound in the rough woollen weave of a tunic that failed to shield Zapata's chest. But as I wander about this hacienda, this hacienda which was filled once upon a revolution with Guajardo's soldiers, I can't help wondering: why wasn't I squashed under their riding boots on the flagstone floor? And then I have this silly idea: why was I not crushed by a toe in the morning if I had crept in to breakfast on one of their socks?

[At this point I laugh out loud, wondering if Disney's Jiminy Cricket is a childhood source of the subject's quaint obsession.]

I share your laughter. I get a chuckle at the idea myself, but the maker and joiner of souls chooses the time and the place to create or dispatch a spirit in one direction or the other.

Did someone tell you about this … what can I call it … 'scheduling' by the maker and joiner of souls? Or is that your own idea?

You know very well whose idea: Martí — the Catalan curandero's.

You and Martí agree that this power picks the exact place and moment where the transmigration or creation of a soul — or, as you put it, crudessence — goes into operation?

We have not discussed this in any detail, but Martí has made such a remark in regard to one of his patients, and I have asked him indirectly if there is a point at which a creature, which we believe doesn't have a soul, gets mixed into the being of one who has. You look up at me like I spat on your empty plate. Yes, sometimes I look at myself as you do now, but at the bottom of my absurd thoughts lies a certainty that I am, in my soul, a cricket, as much now as I was then.

I would love to hear Martí's opinion on this, especially since he says he deals with troubled souls.

Troubled? No, no, no — I am no troubled soul. Since this has had such a happy influence on my life as I live it, I merely wish to identify its true nature.

Okay, I accept your word on that, but why did you not ask Martí to do what I am going to do?

If *they*, those who talk, saw Martí come spend the night here — if those who love smut saw — they might say I am finally letting someone into my closet. An unmarried cabinet minister in a macho country — what might they think I have kept repressed? Homosexuality, some unspeakable deviance or dementia?

[The subject begins to laugh, looking at the plate on which he served me breakfast.] Why are you laughing at my empty plate?

In the old days, there were gay sex workers in two houses at the entrance to the strip that was Cuautla's *zona roja*, its red-light district. They cooked for their clients and left the doors open so the smell might lure others in. Yes, I am laughing at your empty plate because you look like you enjoyed your poor man's chicken, and I note you are sniffing at the black beans, perhaps thinking I will lure you into a seduction like those young gentlemen in the old red-light district. Believe me, you will need a full strong stomach to see you through the night as you watch me go into what my brothers called my mad praying position. My two questions for you to answer are: Do I move my arms and use the palms of my hands? Or do I combine arms, hands, and legs? I should be able to answer the question myself, but my entomological activity happens when I fall into the deepest sleep, past dream, beyond the realm of REM into my other existence, led by the lights of my instinct into action, like the phosphorescent lights of those fish in the deepest dark of the ocean.

It is strange that you have no muscular after-effect of strain in your arms, hands, or legs, which would answer that question for you.

No, I don't have any after-print of intense activity. I only feel refreshed, like my body and soul have had a good night's rest. Growing up with my brothers, I never had a complete night's rest. Worse than the ring of an alarm clock, I woke my brothers. That was all they said when they kicked me out of bed, the two of them, younger than me, angry. They never deigned to touch me with their hands, they preferred to use their feet and kick me out the other side of the bed away from them, afraid perhaps I would slap them with my arms if they pulled me by the legs, kick them if they pulled me by the arms. They told me that much about the violence of my so-called religious mania, which they loathed.

Are there not more logical reasons behind this creature dominating your Id? This is the hacienda where Zapata was assassinated. You live in it. The idea belongs to the place where you live?

No, this is not a suggestion the hacienda has embedded in me. Why do I remember leaping into the blood wound of a martyr at the moment of his assassination, the moment when his last thoughts passed into the ether of eternity and intersected with an insect's instinct to leap, and the simple reflex of the man's body to leap free of the hot lead that pinned him to the earth and into his timeless, indestructible soul?

Can you tell me how you came to be living in the hacienda?

Long after Zapata fell, and after the Revolution ended, the ruin of this hacienda was bought and rebuilt by my father. My father was a bagman for Zapata. He went to the United States, collecting for the cause. Perhaps that is how he learned to accumulate money and deploy it as a banker after the Revolution. He was wily enough to stay in with the power brokers, and after enough time elapsed and he had married my mother (who was much younger than he), admiration for the man brought my father back to the hacienda and to this point of intersection, where the instinct of an insect and the spirit of a man met in the soul plasma of space that attaches to an important place and time. Zapata's mission crossed with this cricket's habit to take a leap into me at that point in time. Like the zafra burns off the chaff, boiling and sweetening the sugar in the cane, when all the green notions of the Revolution were gone, a martyr burned by a bullet sweetened the cause. I became an *abogado*, a lawyer, to serve it. How could I not?

Tell me about that.

I went to UNAM, our National University, then to Harvard. I came back. I set up practice in Cuautla, where the assassin Guajardo was garrisoned many years before. Emiliano's son, Mateo Zapata, was still alive then. Many disputes to be settled were over developers and Indigenous *ejido* land. It began in earnest with Luis Echevarría's presidency, when he dipped into the country's financial pot—until then separate, strong, and untouchable. Echevarría dipped in order to do what he wanted with the money; others dipped into plots of land that were not theirs, land meted out after the Revolution to the people, those *campesinos* who had served in the fighting, with many of the bigger plots left to the widows of the captains and colonels. If they wanted to sell, I sought a fair market price for them; if not, I defended their ownership. The worst cases would be a brother and a sister in dispute over land they held jointly. The brother, an alcoholic, would want to sell for a song and a life in the *pulque cantina*; the sister would know the true value and want to achieve it through the sale. Impatience pitted against patience: the story of Mexico.

In time I became elected as one who worked for the people, having been tested and found trustworthy enough to represent their interests, first in the state's capital, Cuernavaca, then in the country's, Mexico DF.

Why were you at Martí's when I met you? Were you finally there to ask him to do what you have asked me?

You were at the Catalan curandero's to inquire into his spiritual and folk medicine practices. I too meet with him from time to time, and that is why I ran into you. I have always visited him as an important adjunct to the medical community. True curanderos offer a village trinity of trades—physician, psychic, and lay psychiatrist—but my questions to him are more statistical: how many patients or, let's say, ailing souls he meets in a day, a week, a year. I talk to him about possible funding through one of the government's charitable extensions or a non-government organization. I repeat, Martí visiting me here would signal that I am spiritually afflicted—bad publicity for a cabinet minister—while you, on the other hand, are from Spain, an academic who studied at Harvard like myself. Perfectly natural for me to ask you to visit and exchange memories of our alma mater. Still, I cannot say that some higher power or divine calendar did not circle that date when I met you at curandero Martí's.

Martí uses trances to divine his clients' ailments and potential cures.

For his clients, Martí does enter a trance for insight into a cure, but I believe he simply closes his eyes and listens to the *apantle* that runs past his place. You frown at me and think I belittle … that I am mocking Martí and his *apantle*. You do understand our *apantles*, our spontaneous rivers whose waters can't help bursting, like the clearest inspiration, out of the dark earth here. But I can tell you, you'll discover something special in Martí, like you have in my chilaquiles. Stirred into them, you tasted cilantro, epazote, and watercress grown by some very magical *apantles* that sprout from this little hillock a mile or two from Cuautla. They flow in the four directions of the compass, streaming with consolations and cures for the troubled soul.

Just listening to them whisper and sing is enough, but on top of that, I chop my garnishes from there into the chilaquiles. In one way I feed you, and in another infuse you with a taste of wisdom from those blessed *apantles*. As to my spirit, I repeat, it is far from troubled. I am in no way depressed. I am too busy, too preoccupied with work most days to be low. I do not want to rid myself of what has made me the person I am, that gave me this body and soul I have.

What is so good about possessing the soul of a cricket?

It is simply good, like the coffee you are drinking, shade-grown coffee from Tepoztlán. And one cannot deny the music, the call of the field or the hearth. You must have heard them in the cane fields, the mass music of grillos, *de capulines en la caña de azúcar*, or the cricket cheep in the hearth at the fringe of the ashes — as if the soul of the dead fire is singing in the morning. And at night, ah, at night. A line of poetry goes, *La noche es cuando los grillos se convierten en los músicos de amor* — 'Night is when crickets become the musicians of love'. Night-time, when my spirit sings, *you* may hear something I only carry with me in memory every morning. My story is not a Mexican Walt Disney story, where I pop into a charro's pocket and go on a long journey on horseback while the charro, in his spangled tunic, hat, and chaps, sings and swings his lasso at the moon. I am in miniature the dilemma of the werewolf, who wakes naked and never remembers his actions of the night before, only the howl that haunts him.

But what if you do not sleep because I am watching you?

Oh, I will sleep. I am called back to my beginning every night of my life. You may not like watching a naked man take a peculiar position on a wide, wide bed and do a peculiar thing in spiritual — not sexual — orgasm with his host. Meantime, while we have the day, let us take a drive to the Zapata museum in Anenecuilco … but I leap ahead. The cricket in me … ha, but no ha! You may already have visited the museum?

No — my research is in curandero practice, and Zapata was hardly a curandero.

Was he not?

How could he be?

I have drunk of his blood, and his spirit and mine have been lifted up into … what should I call it? A revolutionary communion.

Interesting way to put it, and to be a proper reporter I believe I must suspend my disbelief when it comes to your condition.

I think you are quoting someone, but let us go and see Zapata's drawings and elementary school exercises on the walls of his old home, which we have preserved within the shell of the new Zapata museum.

Well, let's. My car or yours?

My report for Don Fausto Iribás:

As expected, no complete physical transformation takes place. In as true an approximation to the production of a cricket song as any human being might accomplish, your arms move intermittently at a speed so rapid they become a blur while the flats of your hands, your palms, graze each other with a sound like silk singing. The closest comparison I can make is of a finger circling the polished rim of a glass of water or wine: it comes in that peal of one excruciating note for which I must use another comparison. The sound resembles that of a musical saw when someone is playing, and like the saw, your bodily instrument is bent, the action is performed while you are on your knees, your torso arched forward, your head down on the bare mattress, arms raised behind you and high over the nape of your neck, as one sometimes sees in photographs of torture victims. But the action takes place without any display of pain — or, if pain, that of a pleasure so intense it sublimates the sensation the way perfect coitus transmutes the friction of the two physical bodies involved into the purest feeling. The palms of your hands produced for me a flowing, one-note melody, your hands twisted high above the back of your bent head so the palms faced each other in an a cappella song not heard from any choir on earth, except of crickets.

Alejandro Bustos

FEATURE INTERVIEW

George McWhirter

Pulp Literature: *To steal an idea from 'Grillo', what was the moment of this story's crudessence? And what came first, the cricket or Zapata?*

George McWhirter: The answer is that they came together because of where we lived in Mexico: Cuautla in the state of Morelos. After he was murdered, Zapata's body was dragged and dumped in front of Cuautla's Dominican Convent and Church of Santiago Apostol, in the heart of town that was the Guarnación del Sur, where Zapata was the general. Pancho Villa was the general for the northern garrison, the Guarnación del Norte.

Hauled to Cuautla through the countryside from the Hacienda Chinameca, where he was gunned down, his memory permeates the region like the enormous nocturnal chorus of crickets in the cane fields that encompass Cuautla and fill the Valley of Morelos. For me the two merged: Zapata's great assassinated spirit and the music of the crickets, created by millions upon millions of insect musicians. I chose one to be baptized with the spirit of the Revolution in Zapata's blood and to bring those two powerful presences in that part of Morelos together.

PL: *There's something almost Victorian about the way this story is told: through the narration of an outsider to the strange, central drama. I thought of Dr Watson in* *the Sherlock Holmes stories, and Mr Utterson in* The Strange Case of Dr Jekyll and Mr Hyde. *What inspired you to choose an interview format for the story?*

GM: Yes, there is the element of the special investigator in 'Grillo', and a Watson-like storyteller, but the narrator is closer to Poe's old school friend visitor in 'The Fall of the House of Usher', who reports on the prolonged horror that stemmed from two physical defects: a sister's catatonia and a brother's hyperacuity. 'Grillo' needed an outside expert with professional training, relevant experience, a degree from a major institution—all the right fictional credentials—to give the stamp of a professional witness to the observations and affirmation that Don Fausto's aberrant physical behaviour was that of a human-cricket making music in the night.

PL: *Many congratulations on winning this year's prestigious Griffin Poetry Prize for your translation of poet Homero Aridjis's* Self-Portrait in the Zone of Silence! *Like Aridjis's collection, this story pulls threads from everywhere, but especially Mexico's history, current cultural climate, landscape, and myths.*

GM: In 'Grillo', there is definitely an influence from the Mexican, Latin, and North American belief that each of us has an animal spirit. Then there is the other belief perverted by the Aztecs (and, some say, Christians) that you commune with the animal you eat and take on its power, especially by biting into its heart. For 'Grillo', I thought, why wouldn't a symbiosis happen with the insect that ingests the blood of a great human, why might it not take on their spirit, and that spirit migrate into another human … why not?

PL: *Did 'Grillo' grow, at least in part, out of your experience translating Homero's work?*

GM: As a boy, fiddling with a shotgun in an attempt to hit a bird, he shot himself in the stomach. The trauma and an epiphany made him aim his life in the opposite direction to protect all life, and from that he grew into the great campaigner for the environment that he is. El Aridjis Campeador. With Homero, you only need to read the opening poem of *Self-Portrait in the Zone of Silence*, 'El jaguar / The Jaguar', to experience the power of the animal in the human for him. Take the finale. After some verbal peek-a-boo with the jaguar (now you see it, now you don't), we are told … in all the two ways to it … with a cosmic coitus and explosion that the 'jaguar' is in 'you' and 'I':

4
The jaguar that went away
is on its way,

the jaguar that was coming back
still hasn't come

the jaguar of us two
inside you
watches me from outside

5
Our bodies
two solar jaguars
faced off in the night
end clawed up
in the total dawn

You'll see animal–human symbiosis and traces of jaguar in the first stanza of my poem that appeared in the *Abridged Severin* issue out of Derry, Northern Ireland:

Conchita Supervia sings

She sees him in a time of pelts
when animals disguised themselves as men
and men as animals; the better to deceive their prey,
and thus, their faces grew alike: this jaguar-jawed,
young man with feral brows and nose. His gaze
as reposed as a philosopher's

who metronomes the beat of blood in Conchita
Supervia's throat …

PL: *Self-Portrait is not your first translation project. How did an Irish-born Canadian end up translating Mexican poets?*

GM: When I was in a newly created Literary Translation workshop with J Michael Yates and Michael Bullock at UBC's Creative Writing (1969–70), Mike let me know about a new Octavio Paz book-length poem, *Blanco.* I translated *Blanco,* which Octavio liked when I sent it to him. José Emilio Pacheco was in Hispanic Studies at the time, and Mike was gathering together an anthology of the Unofficial Languages of Canada to be called *Volvox.* He wanted me to do some of José Emilio's for it. That was my start with Mexican poets.

So I could work with José Emilio in person after he returned to Mexico, we went to live in Cuautla, where a Mexican friend came from. His mother and father adopted us. They were like grandparents to our kids, and parents to us. They even introduced us to one of Emiliano's sons, Mateo Zapata.

PL: *How does the work of translation compare to that of writing your own poetry and prose?*

GM: When I take a piece in Spanish to that place where there are no words, I see, hear, feel what's there and follow what is going on, then try to put into English what I see, hear, and feel and keep it in track of the action with the same build-ups and climaxes on the line or in the stanza. In one way there's no difference between the two creative processes in making my own poetry and translating it.

PL: *Any advice for would-be translators?*

GM:

1. Assuming you have knowledge of a foreign language, if you don't have a piece of poetry, prose, or drama in that language that haunts you into translating, then go to a good anthology of prose, poetry, or plays in that language and pick a piece you would like to work into English.
2. Next, if you can, find a Literary Translation workshop or group to join.
3. Finally, find a writer whose books haven't been translated. Pick one and write to the publisher, or the writer if they are still alive, for permission to translate and publish.

These are the three things that Emilie Moorhouse did for her translations of Joyce Mansour's *Emerald Wounds* (City Lights, 2023), which Emilie talked about in The Griffin Poetry Prize Translation Talks series on November 13, 2024, which can be visited on YouTube and the Griffin Poetry Prize website.

PL: *Can you tell us what projects you're working on now?*

GM: As to current projects. In brief: pulling all of José Emilio Pacheco's sea poems together (*The Labours of the Sea*); cleaning up a Gabriel Zaid collection (*Questionnaire*) and all of my poems that follow a lifelong relationship (*Espaliered*); also my recent Irish poems (*Now*); and two collections of stories, one set in BC (*Aren't You Glad You're Not Vlad*).

PL: *Thank you for your time, and your strange and wonderful story!*

Select Bibliography

Poetry

The Anachronicles (2008)
The Incorrection (2007), finalist for the Dorothy Livesay Poetry Prize
The Book of Contradictions (2002)
Incubus: The Dark Side of the Light (1997)
A Staircase for All Souls (1996)
Fire Before Dark (1983)
The Island Man (1981)
Twenty-Five (1978)

Queen of the Sea (1976)
Catalan Poems (1971), winner of the 1972 Commonwealth Poetry
  Prize, shared with Chinua Achebe

FICTION

The Gift of Women (2014)
Musical Dogs (1996)
The Listeners (1991)
Cage (1987), winner of the Ethel Wilson Fiction Prize
Paula Lake (1985)
A Bad Day to Be Winning (1984)
Coming to Grips with Lucy (1982)
God's Eye (1981)
Bodyworks (1974)

ANTHOLOGIES (EDITOR)

A Verse Map of Vancouver (2009)
*Where Words Like Monarchs Fly: A Cross-Generational Anthology of Mexican
  Poets in Translation* (1998)
Words From Inside: Prison Arts Foundation (1974, 1975)
Contemporary Poetry of British Columbia, with J Michael Yates and
  Andreas Schroeder (1970)

TRANSLATIONS

Self-Portrait in the Zone of Silence by Homero Aridjis (New
  Directions, New York, 2023), winner of the 2024 Griffin
  Poetry Prize

Poemas Traducidos by Gabriel Zaid (El Colegio Nacional, Mexico, 2 0 2 2)

The Selected Poetry of Gabriel Zaid (Paul Dry Books, Philadelphia, 2 0 1 4)

Tiempo de Angeles / Time of Angels by Homero Ardjis, with contributions by Francisco Toledo (City Lights, San Francisco, 2 0 1 2)

Solar Poems / Poemas Solares by Homero Aridjis (City Lights, San Francisco, 2 0 1 0)

Eyes to See Otherwise / Ojos de Otro by Homero Aridjis (Carcanet Press, 2 0 0 1; and New Directions, New York, 2 0 0 2, with Betty Aridjis)

Jose Emilio Pacheco: Selected Poems (New Directions, New York, 1 9 8 7), winner of the FR Scott Prize for Translation

PLAYS

The House of Bernarda Alba by Federico Garcia Lorca (translation) (Carnegie Centre, 2 0 1 6)

Hecuba by Euripides (translation) (Blackbird Theatre, 2 0 0 9)

Don't Go Walking on the Water (CBC Radio, Vancouver, 1 9 8 1)

The Listeners (CBC Radio, Vancouver, 1 9 8 1)

Now Available!

The magical conclusion to the must-read epic trilogy

the adventures of Allaigna sing

simply a joy to read

keeps you turning pages from beginning to end

an immensely satisfying epic

PULPLITERATURE.COM/ALLAIGNAS-SONG/

THEIR GRANDFATHER'S CHAIR

JM Landels

JM Landels *is the author of the bestselling Allaigna's Song trilogy as well as the spy novel* The Shepherdess, *currently serialized in even-numbered issues of this magazine. 'Their Grandfather's Chair', featuring Allaigna's sisters Branwen and Irdina, takes place during the events of Allaigna's Song: Chorale.*

When she's not writing, editing, or drawing, you can find Jen teaching people to swing swords and ride horses at Academie Cavallo in Langley, BC. You can find @jmlandels on most social media platforms, and at jmlandels.stiffbunnies.com.

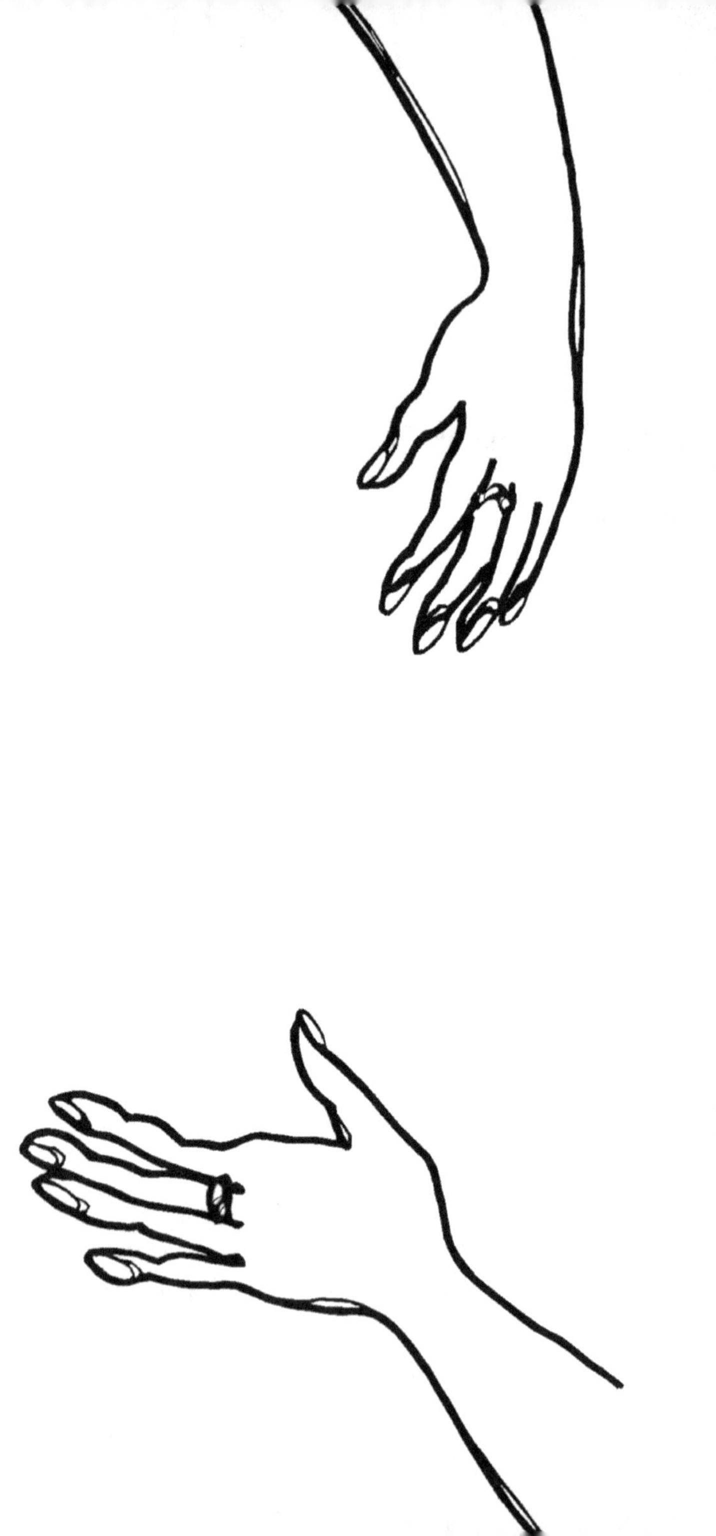

Their Grandfather's Chair
Part 1

Branwen took a deep breath, absorbing all the salt air she could before she and her sister Irdina had to disembark the *Kolmond Lassie*. When they left Teillai, winter had set in, and snow was already a hand-span deep on the ground. Here, the streets that led away from Rheran's port were bare, though the air carried a damp chill.

"At last," muttered Irdina, shouldering past her twin on her way to the gangplank.

This was the first sea voyage for both of them, but Branwen had taken to the sea like a gannet. Irdina, on the other hand, had been ill for most of the ten-day journey from Werrancross to Rheran. At the bottom of the gangplank, Irdina grasped a bollard and leaned over it, shuddering.

Branwen put her hand on her sister's shoulder, in part to comfort, but also to steady her own legs, which still swayed with the movement of the ship. "If you're going to chuck, try to keep it off my shoes this time."

"Fuck you," muttered Irdina, who straightened and flexed her shoulders into place. "I'm starving. Let's find something to eat."

"We're supposed to meet an envoy from the Bastion here." Branwen glanced up at the white stone fortress that dominated the city.

"Well, I don't see one, do you?"

The pier was busy with sailors and dock workers unloading bales of Aerach wool and linen, barrels of apples, and casks of ale, but there was no one in what might be considered palace livery.

"Grandpapa wouldn't forget about us, I'm sure," Branwen said, sounding more confident than she felt. "Angeley wrote him by courier a full week before we left."

Irdina snorted. "Who knows what he would or wouldn't forget. We were four the last time we saw him. I barely remember him."

Just remind him, Angeley had said, *of his family, and his love for you all. And if you can — and only if you can without being noticed — put a few grains of this in his food or drink whenever you have the opportunity.* She had given them each a stoppered vial of pinkish-yellow salts. *But never when Princess Gwannyn is near. Do you understand?*

In that moment Branwen and Irdina both had felt the slight push of compulsion in Angeley's voice: a hint of Leisanmira spellsong that burned her words into their memories.

A carol of bells rang the hour from the towers on either side of the seagate, echoed by more throughout the city.

"Fine," Irdina said, her voice faint and distant behind the bells. "Let's wait another quarter bell, and then make our way to the Bastion. After finding some food."

Branwen, having kept her meals down on board the *Lassie*, was less hungry than Irdina, but after the bells chimed the quarter and another quarter after that, her stomach was rumbling as well. The High Road led straight from the port to the Bastion, but it was an alley off to the east that Irdina veered into, lured by the smell of food that wasn't fish.

Once Irdina got herself around the outside of a meat pie, she was better company. Branwen was still picking at hers — the spices were strange and hotter on the tongue than she was used to.

"Look at all this." Irdina gestured to the maze of market stalls stretching eastward. "Let's shop."

"For what? My pack is heavy enough."

Irdina was thoroughly energized now. "I won't know till I've seen it. But look at all these stalls. Smell the air! Treasures lie this way."

Angeley had given them a half-dozen falcons apiece. For emergencies. "Till the next quarter," Branwen stipulated. She could impose time limits too. "We're supposed to be getting these to Grandpapa, remember?" She patted the two sealed letters in her jerkin pocket. That said, the spicy pie had warmed her innards, and the market was sheltered from the winter wind that funnelled up the High Road. Over the roofs around them, she could still see the pennants of the Bastion announcing that their grandfather the Prince was in residence. As long as they could see those, they wouldn't get lost.

A team of piebald draught horses, napping in their traces, caught Branwen's eye. The Leisanmira wagon was pulled up in front of a long stone trough with a pump at one end. "I'll wait here," she said, drawn by the familiar smell of horses after being at sea for a tenday. She sat on the edge of the trough, near enough to the black-and-white mares to share their companionable rest but not so near as to impinge on their space, while Irdina disappeared between stalls laden with clothing, metalware, books, and jewellery.

The nearest mare turned an inquisitive eye towards Branwen and extended her pink-snipped nose. Branwen put out a hand to let the mare sniff the back of it. "I'm sorry, I have nothing for you."

The mare turned her resigned head back, shifted her hips, and resumed her dozing position. Branwen turned her attention back to the market crowd, watching the green felt hat that kept Irdina's unruly hair in place. She was about to stand to keep better track of her sister, when both horses' heads shot up in unison, and they focused their wide eyes towards the market entrance. A commotion was rippling from the direction of the High Road. Vendors began throwing cloths over the wares and shuttering their stalls.

"Irdina," she called across the crowd, as her sister's hat manoeuvred its way back to her. "What's happening?" she asked of the nearby orange seller, but the woman picked up her basket and hurried away.

She fought against the press of the crowd to get closer to Irdina.

A hand fell on her shoulder. "This way," said a man's voice.

Well-trained by Master Baredh, Branwen's reaction was second nature. She threw her arm straight up, dislodging the man's grip, and turned to send the heel of her other hand into his chin before backing into the chaos of the market.

"Damnit," he said, lunging after her. He caught her by the wrist. "Irdaign sent me."

"Oh!" Branwen managed, as a roll of blue-striped calico hit the man across the back and sent him tumbling onto Branwen.

They fell together, she on her backside and he on his knees. Irdina stood above him, the roll of cloth on its wooden dowel poised for another strike.

"Stop!" Branwen pushed the man out of the way as she regained her feet, placing herself between him and her sister. "He's the envoy." But her words came out in scattered syllables that flew away on a sudden gust of wind.

There was a roar of voices from the crowd around them, but that sound too seemed to be picked up and carried away. In its place a silence fell, like giant flakes of snow that drifted in front of her face. It interrupted Irdina's voice, the clamour of the crowds, and the words of the envoy, till the market was quiet as a winter night. And yet the bodies around her still moved in a frantic tide. A huge man pushed past her, sending her stumbling deeper into the crowd, separating her from her sister once more.

She called in her loudest voice, but it was muffled to nothing by the cloying silence. She was no mage, but she knew enough about magic to feel it clinging to her skin, filling her mouth and ears, making it seem as if she couldn't breathe.

And then the crowd parted like a river around an island. In the centre of that island walked a tall woman clothed in black, her skin only a shade lighter than her garb. Her eyes were amber, like those of Irdina's buckskin mare, and magic swirled around her like water. Her yellow gaze passed over Branwen, and the ring Angeley had given her prickled and burned like it was fresh out of the forge. Branwen stood on her tiptoes to look over the heads of the rushing crowd, wondering if Irdina's half of the puzzle ring also burned under her glove.

The woman strode past, then stopped and spun around. The skirts of her black cloak whirled in slowed time. She fixed Branwen with her buckskin eyes, and said something Branwen couldn't parse through the dense silence accumulating between them. The mage's long legs carried her back to Branwen in two strides, and the silence scattered in her wake, letting syllables of sound through in meaningless pops and clicks. The woman removed her black glove and reached a long finger out to touch Branwen on the chin.

Sound flooded back like water poured from a bucket. Through the shouts and clamour of people in flight, the mage's voice shot arrow-straight to Branwen's ears. "Name and abode."

The voice was so compelling that Branwen had to fight back her true name. But the ring burned on her finger, its pain cutting through the arcane compulsion. "Isha," she forced out. "Cooper. Of Werrancross."

"You came off the *Kolmond Lassie*."

Branwen nodded, feeling the painful, sparking static of her ring fighting off the sharp force of the woman's arcana.

The Mageguard — for that was undoubtedly what she was — motioned to one of the two men accompanying her. "She's not the one, but she's been in her company. Take her for questioning."

Branwen opened her mouth to protest, but the flakes of silence flew around her head once more, choking the sound in her mouth. The man grabbed her wrist and slapped it with a short leather strap. The leather clung to her wrist like a living thing. She clawed at it with her other hand, but could find no end to the strap: it was an unbroken circle.

"This way." His words were far away and indistinct, but were now the only sounds she could hear through the muffled silence.

When he took her by the elbow, all her fighting instinct vanished like the sounds, and she followed him, meek as a collared hound, to the wall of the nearest building. He lifted her hand above her head and pressed her wrist to the wall.

"Stay there," he said.

He was speaking not to her, but to the leather band. And it obeyed. He walked off into the crowd and she remained, her hand stuck to the wall high above her head.

She twisted as far as she could, turning beneath her arm to face outward, though she had to stand on her tiptoes and the leather pulled at her skin. The square was almost empty now, barrows and handcarts shuttered or wheeled away. There was no sign of Irdina or of the man who'd accosted them.

The other Mageguard man had two more people in tow, leather wrapping their wrists as well. She recognized them both. The short man, with a head like a smooth brown egg and white carpet of beard, was the ship's mate, or boatswain, or some other nautical rank Branwen hadn't bothered to learn. The other, a well-dressed woman—Saradi was her name—was a wool merchant who had disembarked when she and Irdina had.

Branwen's two shipmates would corroborate her false identity, for she had been using that name on board. But, she wondered, was that the name that would serve her best?

Her captor's voice eked through the melting silence. "Here."

Her wrist came away from the wall so suddenly she stumbled forward, nearly colliding with him. She composed her face, brushed her clothes down, and stood at her tallest, imagining her mother at her most indignant. The silence seemed to fall away, pooling at her feet.

"Do you know who I am?" she demanded.

"Isha Cooper, of Werrancross." The amber-eyed woman appeared at her subordinate's shoulder, her gaze penetrating.

"That is what you told me, and the passenger manifest will agree, will it not?"

With her left hand, Branwen reached into the inner pocket of her coat and produced one of the sealed letters she'd carried from home, hoping it was the right one. Her sense of dread heralded a warning, but she felt she had no choice. She offered the letter to the woman, relieved to see it was the single-sealed letter of introduction.

The Mageguard studied the seal and waved her hand over the letter. Even through the parchment and her glove, Branwen could feel her ring tingle at the magic. Apparently satisfied there were no charms upon the letter, the Mageguard took it from her and cracked the seal. She tipped her chin sideways, appraised Branwen from head to toe, then nodded.

"Release her," she said to her subordinate. With no hint of apology to Branwen, she added, "Since we are taking these suspects to the Bastion, we will give you an escort there."

Branwen opened her mouth to protest, to say she needed to find her sister, but a seed of caution stopped her. Instead, she replied, "Thank you for that generous offer. But I am travelling with a companion. We became separated when …" She prevented herself from saying *when you panicked the crowd*. "… in the confusion. I must find her."

"Give me something of hers, and we will set a search ward."

Branwen shook her head. "I have nothing." This was true. Though she was fairly certain that, in the hands of a mage, the half of the puzzle ring she carried could be used to find Irdina's. But Angeley's instructions had been clear: *do not either of you remove it from your fingers, except to put it in the hand of your sister.*

The woman was losing patience. "Then her name and a description. Be quick."

"Wenna Cooper," she gave Irdina's shipboard name. "She comes to about my shoulder, with gold hair, straighter than mine. She's wearing a blue hood." None of it described Irdina or her clothes at all, but it was a passable description of their older sister Lauriana. "Please," Branwen continued, "I welcome your help, but I think I can find her best myself." This was true. She knew Irdina as well as she knew her own right hand. Knew where she'd go and the choices she'd make. And knew that her sister would disappear at the sight of Mageguard.

"I am sorry, but I can't allow that. His Highness your grandfather would have my hide if I allowed anything to happen to you." She bared her teeth in a chilling smile. "And there is a murderer, still loose in the city, who came off your ship. We will get you safe to the Bastion and find your companion."

Branwen looked at the ground while she weighed her choices, and her chances of slipping away from three mages in the empty square. Irdina was resourceful, and had her own letter of introduction. At last she raised her chin. "Thank you for your assistance. I appreciate the escort." She held her hand out for the letter, and was surprised when the Mageguard surrendered it with a bob of the head.

Irdina lifted the roll of calico, preparing to strike again at the man who'd assaulted them. Branwen's shout reached her ears, and then the sound washed away. But it was enough to make her hesitate. And that was time enough for the red-headed man to scramble to his feet and put space between them.

His mouth moved, but no sound came out. His posture, though — hands in front, fingers spread wide — was one of appeasement, or at least truce. Irdina stayed her hand, but brought the cloth roll in front of her, holding it like a two-handed sword, point on line to keep the man at bay while she cast her gaze for a glimpse of Branwen.

But the strange, silent, rushing crowd had carried her sister away. Irdina vacillated as she tried to assess the greatest threat: the crowd that had separated them, the unearthly silence — no doubt arcane — or the man who had accosted them. The last was probably the least, but it was the closest at hand. She felt her anger, never far from the surface, uncoil and erupt from her mouth in an incoherent surge. At the same time she stamped her foot and jabbed toward the man in front of her. It was a feint, meant to threaten, not strike.

Which is why she was startled into renewed silence when the man staggered backward as if punched in the stomach. And the sound . . . the sound of her yell had existed, if only for a moment, amid the smothering silence.

She was about to follow it forward and press the man further back when she felt a cool finger touch the back of her neck.

"Be still," said a voice as calm and soft as steel. The voice came not through her ears, which were blocked by the silence, but through the bones of her skull and the rush of her blood.

And Irdina, rather than spinning to engage this new assault, let the bolt of cloth fall. She watched it bounce and roll toward the redhead, who stepped over it. He seemed to move in jerky, quick time. From the corner of her eye Irdina saw a hand, lumpy with age, reach toward Redhead and grasp his wrist. His movements slowed, and his image sharpened.

The rushing crowd, meanwhile, moved at inhuman speed, blurring like water over a fall. Then, like water disappearing into the cracks on dry ground, it vanished, leaving behind a black-clad trio and two figures she recognized from the ship. And behind them, Branwen.

Irdina's half of the puzzle ring burned as she tried to step forward.

The voice from behind her repeated, more firmly this time, "Be still."

The movements of the figures in front of her eyes became more jerky, skipping from beat to beat like a dropped-word song. Was that Branwen's letter of introduction she handed over? To a Mageguard? Was she a prisoner? Branwen looked straight at Irdina and seemed not to see her. And then they left, zipping like water fleas towards the market entrance.

Irdina fought to follow, her ring burning, anger balling up in her chest again. The light touch of the finger at the base of her neck lifted, and the ground seemed to shudder and shift beneath her feet.

"By the stars, girl, you're strong," said the voice.

Irdina spun in anger, hand raised, poised to strike or defend. The person before her was tiny, bent with age, and, from the pale blue cast to her eyes, nearly blind.

Irdina couldn't hit an old woman, but the man beside them clearly thought she might. He stepped between them. Him, she had no qualms about striking. But he was young, fit, and taller than she. For once, prudence bested anger and she took two quick steps backward, stumbling on the cloth roll.

The urge to stay and confront these two was strong, but the pull of her sister was stronger. Irdina turned her rage to speed, racing towards the square's eastern entrance.

With each step up the hill, Branwen felt the tangible distance between herself and her sister grow. They had of course been farther apart than this before — sometimes for a week or more when one or the other accompanied their mother or nurse on trips to Aleran, Doniver, or Rillonna. But in a strange city, in a foreign principality—no matter that it was ruled by their grandfather—a distance of half a league and half a bell seemed immeasurably large.

The gates of the Bastion were imposing—twice the height of Osthegn's—with thick towers on either side. Not as tall as the towers of the seagate they'd sailed through this morning, but round and impenetrable. The Mageguard who had stuck her wrist to the wall now escorted her through the sally port and into the yard, with no show of deference but at least no hostility. He marched across the yard to the inner doors of the keep while the other Mageguard took the merchant and the sailor to the opposite side of the yard. The woman Mageguard had left them long before they reached the Bastion.

"Porter!" bellowed her escort.

A square man in palace livery opened the door a crack, and then widened it with a bow as he recognized the Mageguard.

"Your eminence," he said with a puzzled tone. "What brings you to this door?"

"Honoured guest," the Mageguard replied. "Take her to the audience room and alert His Highness's chamberlain."

Back on the crowded high street, people and animals moved with none of the panic that had filled the square only a few moments earlier. But there, halfway up the long hill, was the black-clad trio, the prisoners, and Branwen, made visible by the wide berth they were given.

Irdina felt a wave of panic propel her up the street. But Redhead was beside her again, like a horsefly that just won't leave one alone. He wisely did not put a hand on her shoulder this time, but he angled himself into her path.

"You don't want to be following that lot," he said. "Mageguard."

"I know," she said, turning the fear brimming in her eyes to anger. "But my sister is with them."

"Voluntarily or not, do you think?"

"I don't know." She focused her anger, turning it to a cold ball in her throat that forced down tears. "I hate them," she whispered, more to herself than to him.

Because of Mageguard, her mother and her oldest sister, the latter only just returned home, were lying at death's lintel. And it was because of Mageguard that she and Branwen had been sent here, across the sea from their home to spy on their own grandfather. To see how deep he lay within the mages' webs, and to start to unravel them. The anger spun and roiled in her throat as she reminded herself of the weight of that task on her fourteen-year-old shoulders.

"I'm Glaignen." Redhead's words broke her out of her building fury. "I was to meet you at the docks, but they"—he nodded towards the retreating figures—"were about. I'm sorry we got off on the wrong foot." He extended a hand, palm forward in the Leisanmira greeting.

Her well-trained manners managed to squeeze past the anger and she met his palm with hers. "I'm sorry I hit you."

He lifted a shoulder. "I'd say no harm done, but had you not, I think your sister might be with us now."

A bubble of the anger, at herself as much as him, escaped. "You shouldn't go around putting hands on people unawares, then." Her voice crept louder in spite of herself.

His got lower. "Let me show you another way to the

Bastion. With fewer blackcoats in it. But first, Nourd would like a word."

Branwen's first impulse was to say no, with a swear word or two for emphasis. But the names *Nourd* and *Glaignen* finally settled in the front of her brain as those Angeley had given. She nodded, not taking her eyes off of the retreating figures of her sister and the Mageguard.

He held out a hand. "Come. We know exactly where they're going. You'll not lose her."

She didn't take the hand, but she did follow him back into the market square, which was starting to fill again. There, as if they had never been elsewhere, was the vardo and the team of piebald mares. Glaignen led her to the back and opened the door, gesturing for her to enter.

"After you," she said.

To his credit, he showed not a whit of temper at her reluctance. He swung into the dark doorway of the vardo, skipping the two steps.

Caught between hurry and caution, Irdina stood on the top step and leaned in, a hand on each side of the door frame as she waited for her eyes to adjust to the dark interior. Glaignen was already at the front of the tiny room on wheels, leaning into a cupboard of sorts. Intrigued, Irdina came further in, ducking under the dim orange evenlamp that hung from the ceiling. The cupboard was in fact a bed, with sliding doors. Inside, the old woman reclined, her frizzy white hair spread out like a milkweed puff on the pillows behind her.

"I'm fine, Glaignen," came her voice, dry and light as milkweed down itself—nothing like the forceful, stony voice that had reverberated through Irdina's skull earlier. "Kolluk'kan is growing stronger. Or I'm growing weaker. It was hard to hide an extra person, that's all." Irdina could feel a stab of disapproval with Glaignen's quick look towards her. "Put the kettle on, love."

"Grandmother," said Glaignen, standing as tall as he could under the low ceiling. "I've brought Irdina."

"Well then, put enough water on for three." The voice like round stones was back. "Come here, girl, let me see your face."

Irdina obeyed. There was the same quality to Nourd's voice as to Angeley's. It brooked no argument. Still, the ball of anger in Irdina's throat began to spin again as she knelt by the box bed.

"Tt. Don't waste your anger here, child," Nourd said. "It's a mighty force. Save it for when you need it."

Nourd's voice was so reasonable, so calm, that Irdina's anger spun faster. But she held it back, clenched behind her teeth. The old woman gave a wry smile, and Irdina knew Nourd could still see it somehow, despite those milky eyes.

"We've met before — do you remember?"

Irdina shook her head, then added, in deference to the clouded eyes, "I don't, I'm sorry."

"You were very small, your sister and you. No more than three, I'd think. Your" — there was a pause — "nurse brought all of you to me at one point or another. Except wee Vardry — I've yet to meet him. But that's neither here nor there. Forgive the ramblings of an old woman.

"You were both so strong, you and Branwen. Even at three. But you are stronger together." She gave a little cough and sank back against the pillows. "Give me your hand," she said, her voice weak as milkweed down once more.

Irdina complied anyway, and took the woman's cold dry hand in her own. Nourd lay in silence while guilt trickled into

Irdina's heart. It was her fault. Her anger had made the old woman work harder than necessary to conceal them from the Mageguard. And her anger had caused the scuffle that had separated her from Branwen. She closed her eyes to stop her guilt from showing, and to keep the anger down.

"Let it go," whispered Nourd. "You don't need it now. Breathe it out."

Light as they were, Nourd's words passed into Irdina like the faintest breeze. She felt the hard, shiny ball of anger soften at the edges.

"Let me borrow it, child," said Nourd. "There is always more where it came from."

With that, the ball softened all the way through, to a liquid she could no longer trap behind her throat. It flowed through her, out the soles of her feet and the tips of her fingers. She felt Nourd's other hand on top of hers, warm now. She opened her eyes as Nourd sat up.

"Thank you, child," she said in her smooth marble voice. "Your anger will always be there for you when you need it. But it is painful to carry around all the time."

This was an error, thought Branwen. She should have refused to be escorted here to the Bastion. She was no criminal. She was the granddaughter of the Prince, and more, a citizen of Aerach. There were several seats in the small audience chamber, but there was one set higher than the rest. She took off her gloves, her pack, and her winter coat, and placed them on a lesser chair. As she rubbed her chin, the puzzle ring tingled, but she was too deep in thought to pay it much heed. She sat in her grandfather's chair to wait.

§

To be continued in Pulp Literature *Issue 46, Spring 2025.*

For more high fantasy, family drama, and political intrigue set in the lands of the Ilmar, check out the spellbinding Allaigna's Song trilogy from JM Landels at Pulp Literature Press. https://pulpliterature.com/allaignas-song/

PHOLOE

Dan MacIsaac

Dan MacIsaac is a poet from Metchosin, BC. Recently, his poetry has appeared in literary journals such as Event, Juniper, Stand, and Canadian Literature. Brick Books published his poetry collection, Cries from the Ark. His work was shortlisted for the Walrus Poetry Prize, The Nick Blatchford Occasional Verse Contest, and the CBC Short Story Prize. Dan's historical short story, 'Crossroads', was featured in Pulp Literature Issue 32, Autumn 2021. His website is www.danmacisaac.com.

$\mathcal{P}$HOLOE

Seizing me from
my craggy island,
Aeneas tore me
like a lush fig.

My body scented
his bed until
he was seduced
by the mad queen.

He forgot
my grey eyes,
my glowing flesh,
my quick fingers.

Cast off, I became
the last place prize,
an urn for slops or
ash, handed over

to the loser who
had crippled his
craft, splintering
every oar.

My twin sons,
half-Cretan
demi-beasts,
will answer for me.

Born captive like dogs,
they will claim
a dark blood-right,
kin to blind Cupid,

the most treacherous god,
and howl down
from the burnt hills
to gnaw Trojan bones.

Note: In Virgil's epic, callous Aeneas cast off his Cretan slave, giving her as a prize to a mariner who had run aground and finished dead last in the Trojan boat race.

THE PAST AS FOUNDATION FOR THE FAMILY HOME

Shelley Lavigne

Shelley Lavigne *is a purveyor of moist literature, usually queer horror. They live in Ontario, where they roam their neighbourhood in search of haunted houses and cool bugs. You can also find them online at shelleylavigne.com.*

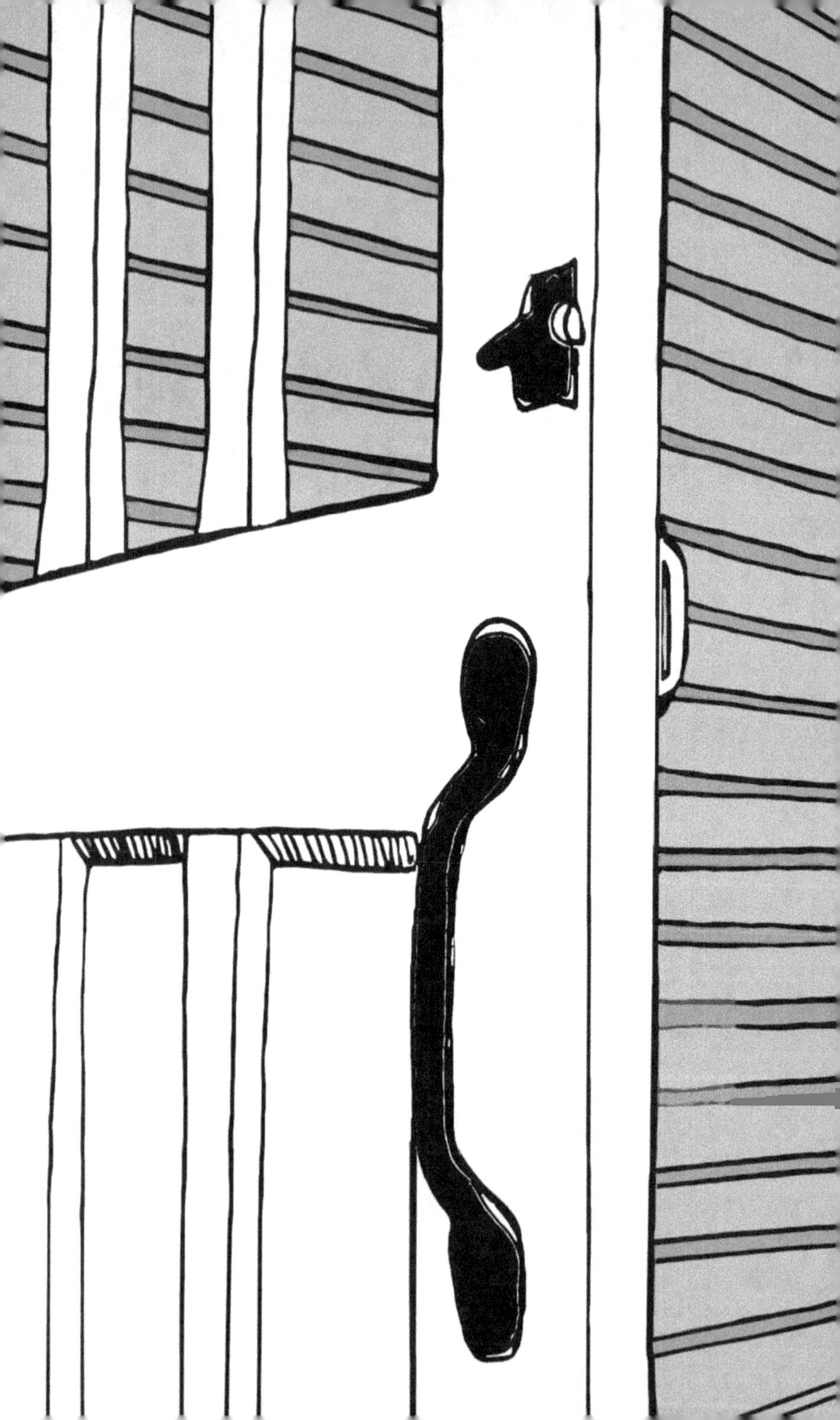

The Past as Foundation for the Family Home

CW: Mentions of self-harm and suicidal ideation, borderline abusive family dynamics

Entryway

My parents' text arrives after they do, the first time slip of the day. *We're almost there,* followed by a string of emojis: a car, fireworks, a martini glass. Whoever taught my mother to use the emoji keyboard was either a nuisance or the best person who ever lived, depending on my mood.

We stand, crowded, in the entryway. Four adults, a baby bump, and way more luggage than a couple normally needs for a weekend. I hope this doesn't mean they intend to stay longer than we agreed.

"I love what you've done with the place," my mother says, touching the plaster patch where there used to be a key hook. "It's already changed so much, it's like we never even lived here. How easily thirty-seven years can be completely erased."

"It's just a start," Rita says, either unaware of the insult or ignoring it. "We'd love to eventually put down Maltese tiles, bring in some of my family history."

"Putting down tile, that's a big job," my father says.

He laid the current tiles sometime in the eighties, a weird, patchy yellow-brown that looks like shit spread thin.

"Well, Riley is quite handy," my wife says, placing a hand on my lower back, small circles telling me that she knows I am tense. I relax into it. *I* should be giving *her* a back rub — Rita's has been paining her all morning, but I'm not about to stop her. "You raised them right," she says with a smile.

"I'm not sure what's wrong with these tiles. I nearly broke my back laying them."

My mother silences him with a hand on the neck, likely rubbing those same circles Rita is rubbing into me. Is that where Rita got the idea, or where I got the habit?

"Well, let's not all just stand here. How about we get settled in, and then you can take us for a tour? Show us all the *modifications* you've made," my mother suggests.

"You'll be in my old room," I tell my parents, as I pick up the largest bag.

CHILDHOOD BEDROOM

I swung open the door and flicked on the boombox, drowning out my mother with the angry, horny sounds of Green Day.

On the bed, a dress.

The one my mother wanted me to wear to my aunt's wedding. It looked like a cross between a pastry and something a little girl would use for princess dress-up — pink, purple, and glittery with a poofy skirt filled with—oh, Satan—an actual hot-pink crinoline.

"It's a nice dress," my mother said. "I don't get why you won't wear it."

Because I'd feel like a doll in it.

Because I hated dresses and everything associated with them.

If they were on others, then that was fine. But on me? No way! And if I could respect other's clothing choices, why couldn't they respect mine?

Life was so incredibly unfair.

"Your cousins will be there. Don't you want to make a good impression?" The doorknob rattled in my hand and I held it tight to keep it from turning. Her voice came through the thin door easily, as if she was already in there with me. I had to keep that from happening. "You need to grow up if you want me to let you make your own decisions."

"I can't grow up unless you start respecting my decisions."

"Your brain isn't fully formed yet, trust me. I was a real idiot too when I was your age."

The knob rattled harder but I held on, jamming my foot against the bottom of the door for extra protection.

"You're acting really mature, Riley! Open up!"

I knew I didn't have long before my father came home from work. He'd get the door opened no problem. I had to get her off my case before then. So I'd have to lie, even if I hated it. I carefully crossed my fingers, never losing grip on the knob.

"I'll get changed, promise."

I felt a tremor in the doorknob as she let go. "Being treated as an adult won't happen until you start acting like one. And being an adult means understanding that you have to put others ahead of yourself sometimes."

I heard her step away thinking she had won.

I could just imagine her victorious little smirk.

I'll show her, I thought, as I walked to my closet. I had some neckties in there I could probably fashion into a noose. Have fun getting a corpse into that crinoline monstrosity!

CLOSET

"Well, it's really strange to be sleeping here," my mother says.

I blink hard. The closet is empty except for wire hangers that clack gently in the breeze of the opening door.

"Without the carpet, the floor is cold. Do you have some slippers?" my father asks.

A headache circles my head like a cartoon bird, a tingle on my scalp indicates that a migraine is not far behind. The sudden shift in time feels like surfacing too fast from underwater, nitrogen bubbling in my veins. It's been a while since I've had an episode.

My mother fixates on every small change, as if the threadbare orange carpet had been anything but musty and dated. As if the new entryway isn't a nice thing to come home to instead of that gloomy, wood-panelled tunnel of dread and bad memories.

"Being back here, it's bringing back the good old days. Remember how your dad used to do impressions of YuckYuck the clown to calm you down after you had nightmares? Oh, and where did you put your swimming trophies? You were such an impressive swimmer, it's a shame you never kept it up."

Oh, gosh, reminiscing. Why did she think those were fun memories? Maybe because she hadn't been hazed for the high school swim team. Nor did she need to calm me down from the night terrors I still suffered from on occasion.

I'm in for a bad weekend.

"Is this one of those new foam beds?" my father asks, testing the mattress by attempting to bounce on it. "I don't know if I'll be comfortable on one of these."

"Your dad has a bad back," my mom supplies as she hangs her clothes. As if I haven't heard that for most of my life. An Avril Lavigne poster grins menacingly down at her. *Same, Avril.*

"You'll be comfortable. They're really fancy."

To be honest, they were cheap, and with a kid on the way it seemed like the best option.

My mom frowns at me, an indication that my tone is sharp. My headache gets worse.

"Once you're done, head down to the living room. I just need to grab some headache pills."

Bathroom

I approached the mirror, got in really close. So close my breath clouded the surface. So close that I could only see my face—not the body that was changing in ways I hated. If I got close enough, all I would see were the pores filled with sebum, the angry scabbed mess across my forehead. I pressed my indexes to a swollen one, excising impurities from myself.

I flicked on the bathroom fan to drown out the fighting I could hear from downstairs.

I didn't want to know.

I found another big zit.

This I could control, this was fine. Sure, the scars were visible, more so than things you could hide with bracelets. But it was not as destructive, not as prone to infection, not as long-lasting. Just a little release, not a permanent one.

"Are you picking at yourself again?" my mother asked from the other side of the door. I had been so sucked in that I hadn't heard her coming upstairs.

"I'll be right out," I said, splashing water on my face, but I knew it wouldn't help. She'd know what I had been up to — my swollen, red face would give it away.

It's better than the other option, I wanted to tell her.

"Hurry up!"

Staircase

My mother stood halfway up the stairs, rearranging the pictures in the staircase to make space for the tenth-grade school picture she'd put in an ostentatious gilt frame. She'd frowned and sighed when she'd pulled it out of the envelope. I had hoped it would be buried in the kitchen junk drawer but here it was: my metallic smile, the frizzy hair, the patchy skin, the clear discomfort and wrongness of my face.

"Why do these always turn out so bad?" she asked as she spotted me.

Did she need to dig it in? Weren't parents supposed to be nice?

"Why even buy them if you think I look hideous?"

"I don't …" She sighed. "It's the photographers, not you. You'll see, one day you'll want these pictures, you'll want to show your kids how you looked when you were their age. And you'll be surprised that you used to look this young. I should show you mine sometime. Gosh, it really brings back memories looking at them. Those were the days!"

I passed her on the stairs, not making eye contact with the other dozens of me on the wall.

Living room

My mother didn't need to say it, but she did anyway. Perhaps she'd heard it on one too many shows and it was just automatic.

"I'm not angry, I'm just disappointed."

"After everything we've done," my father added.

I failed to see the relevance but was aware of his temper and so looked between mother and Rita, trying to figure out my path forward. Everyone seemed to be waiting for my tongue to become unstuck.

"I don't really think this has anything to do with you," I finally said. It was the truth. But my father's face turned red. High blood pressure—it killed grandfather last year.

"People will talk. Folks don't like things that aren't … usual. I have a business—have you ever thought of my business? I might lose clients over this kind of thing. And then, what? Your mom would have to go back to work? Or I'd have to work handyman jobs. I'm not in the shape I used to be."

Rita fidgeted with the straps of her dress. It had been on the floor when mother walked in on us earlier, and there was very little room for interpretation as to what we had been doing.

"I love her, Mother," I said, taking Rita's hand.

"And what do *your* parents think of that? I can't imagine they'd be thrilled to find out their daughter's a—"

My father stopped himself there.

I felt Rita's hand tighten in mine, and my mother stepped between my father and me.

"You're just too young to be sure about this kind of thing. It's just a phase, nothing worth ruining the whole family over," my mother said as she stepped over to my father, rubbing circles into his back.

When she spoke again, she did so with a voice that trembled.

"We love you very much, sweetheart," my mother said. "You're just making a silly mistake. One day we'll all just look back over this whole thing and laugh."

"Rita isn't a mistake."

"If you can't respect our rules, then get out of my house!" my father yelled.

I grabbed Rita's hand and ran.

FRONT HALLWAY

I fall back into the hall, a stumble that bangs my head on the frames Rita hung earlier this week.

"I'm going to get us some drinks," I wheeze out, fighting the urge to run out of the house like we did that day, taking refuge at Rita's until my parents calmed down.

"Don't take too long, we're parched!"

I resist the urge to tell them they barely spent thirty minutes on the road. That this was their house once and they can just serve themselves; that it feels weird having them back here; that this no longer feels like my home but some sort of cairn of memories.

"We had such great times in this house!" I hear my mother exclaim.

And yet all I can remember right now are the bad ones. I wonder if she's thinking of a different home, a brighter home than this shadow I'm standing in.

Kitchen

"I'm going to eat you out in our eat-in kitchen," I said. Rita laughed and playfully nudged my shoulder, dodging my kiss.

"How are you a horn-dog all the time?" Nonetheless, she sat up on the table, legs spread.

I knelt in front of her, nibbling on the meat of her thigh before pushing up her dress.

"I'm the cookie monster," I said with a laugh, doing my best impression. Which wasn't that great, if I was being honest. "I'm going to eat your cookie."

"People are going to *eat* on this table."

"And it'll be our dirty, *dirty* little secret."

Dining room

"Are you okay?" Rita stands next to a flat-packed table we have yet to assemble. "You've been in there for a while."

I touch her face, feel the swell of her stomach. It's the same as it was this morning. I'm in the present, or close enough to it. Rita looks worried. I know she's about to ask me whether I've taken my meds, and I know she'll count them tonight to make sure. I hate the way I make her anxious sometimes. That sometimes the thing I most need to protect her from is me. That sometimes I'm just stuck in the past, where she can't get to me.

"It just feels weird to have them back here," I say. At least this last memory was a good one. But it wasn't *now*.

"I know what you mean. But I'm so thankful for what they did. We would never have a home without them, we'd still be stuck in that little one-bedroom. So, if they impose on us a bit, it's okay. And if you want to scream at them, hold it in and let it out when they go. Okay?"

Rita is so patient and kind that I'm never quite sure how I managed to find her and keep her. I want to sob and I want her to hold me. I want to shrink to the size of an infant so she can embrace and protect me, give me a different past than the one that is impregnated in these walls.

"It just feels like this place is so full of awful memories sometimes."

"It's not all bad, though. We kissed for the first time in your room, and remember how your mom spent all day making you that black forest cake when you turned thirteen even though she hates baking? It was so good. Then she made us another when we got married and it reminded me of that day, the big smile on your face when you took your first bite. The past isn't just good or bad." I shrug, but she takes my hands and leads me back to the kitchen. "Let's make new memories to wallpaper over the past."

Nursery

"She's finally sleeping," Rita will say as I enter the room.

A mobile in the shape of the solar system will spin slowly behind her, giving her a planetary halo, like she's the goddess of the universe. In her arms will rest a child I will love so much it will feel like a pain in my chest.

"She snores kind of like you," Rita will say as I cuddle close and kiss her temple.

Just like Rita will be attuned to the smallest sound Mia makes, I'll hear the muted buzz of a phone call. No one but my mother would call at this time. Rita won't hear it, but she will feel me tense for a moment.

"Stay with me, spend a bit more time here."

BABA YAGA AND THE BEAR

Gregg Chamberlain

Gregg Chamberlain lives in rural Ontario, Canada, with his missus, Anne, and their cats, who let the humans think they are in charge. He writes speculative fiction and poetry for fun. One example of his fun, 'The Monster Hunter', appeared in Pulp Literature Issue 10, Spring 2016. Several dozen other examples have appeared in Abyss & Apex, Ares, Daily Science Fiction, Polar Borealis, Weirdbook, and other magazines, along with various anthologies. He also does zombie filk rewrites of traditional nursery rhymes and campfire songs, just because he can and to showcase his strange sense of humour..

$\mathcal{B}$ABA YAGA AND THE BEAR

As told to Gregg Chamberlain

Is it true? Is it so? Maybe yes, maybe no. Don't ask me, I do not know. But this is how I heard the story go.

It was once upon a day, when the skies were grey, with cloudy gloom for the afternoon so the warm sunlight could not shine so bright. That is when the good Baba Yaga stepped out of her little izba to look upon her garden.

Yes, that's right, I say 'the good Baba Yaga', for that is the proper and respectful way to speak of the most powerful witch there is, was, or ever will be in all the worlds. Baba Yaga has eyes so sharp and ears so keen that she can hear the merest whisper of a word, good or ill, spoken about her, and also see who spoke the word. What would she do then? Ah, that would depend upon the word that is spoken.

Still, that is nothing for you or me to worry about, for we will say nothing but good things about Baba Yaga, whose mood upon that afternoon of which the story tells was as grim as the grey overcast sky. The old witch's dour look was truly dire to behold as she cast an eye over the rows of plants in the 'medicinal' corner of her garden.

The lips of her mouth twisted for a moment into a thin smile as she looked upon bunches of blooming belladonna.

"Nice," she murmured.

The pointed petals of the flowers perked up at the sound of her voice, and spread open wider in appreciation of the wise woman's praise.

Baba Yaga moved a couple of steps further along the mounded rows of the garden. Her face clouded over as she surveyed the miserable-looking monkshood. The corners of her mouth sank down, and thick frown lines bumped up against the wrinkles of her face.

"*Gavno*," she muttered.

The leaves of the monkshood drooped and its blue-purple flowers wilted at the contempt in the old witch's voice.

Baba Yaga glared down at the pathetic patch of monkshood. "I will see *you* looking much better soon," she said. "This is so, yes?"

Petals quivered and leaves fluttered as each and every monkshood plant straightened to attention in immediate agreement.

Nodding with satisfaction, Baba Yaga moved on to inspect her collection of toadstools just as chattering teeth sounded loud behind her.

Turning, Baba Yaga looked towards the fence of pale-white thigh-bones that surrounded her hut and garden. The skulls mounted atop the fence stakes rattled against each other. The *clack-clack-clack* of their bony jaws almost shook loose the teeth in their sockets.

A black cat sauntered out through the open doorway of the hut, sat down on the step, and began licking at one paw.

"We have a visitor," said the cat, pausing for just a moment to look towards Baba Yaga and then starting to lick at the other paw.

Beyond the bleached-bone barrier, a little path ambled away down a gentle slope and across a little clearing to the edge of a great dark forest of old pine and ancient oak that separated Baba Yaga's home from the rest of the world. Every skull on its fence post was turned towards that forest, their empty eye sockets filling with a soft white glow as they watched for the arrival of a visitor to the izba of Baba Yaga.

The wise woman's eyes narrowed as someone emerged from the wood. Her long thin nose lifted, and she inhaled deeply from the sudden breeze that blew up the hillside towards her.

"*Tfu! Tfu! Tfu!*" Baba Yaga spat three times on the ground, chuckling out loud to herself. "Nowadays the odour of Russia is everywhere throughout the whole wide world. But this one smell I know very well. In the old days, this one, and many others before him, would come to me with word of the will and wants of tsars and commissars. But that was long and long ago. There are no more tsars, and Stalin and little Nikita rest in their unquiet graves now. The days are past when the so-called 'masters of the world' remembered and respected Baba Yaga. So why does *he* come now, I wonder, to my little hut?"

With eyes that could see both sides of a kopek a hundred metres away, she watched as a bald-headed man made his way along the path to the little izba. His approach was slow, Baba Yaga noted, almost reluctant, like that of an unwilling messenger bearing bad news or, even worse, a foolish demand.

"Ho! Ivan Ulyanovich Dzhansky, the years have come and

gone since last you came to visit me." Baba Yaga smiled as the man startled and stopped a moment on the path.

"You know me?"

Baba Yaga laughed, a harsh cachinnation that echoed to and fro across the clearing. She tapped a skinny finger against her thin nose and grinned. "I would know the stench of you anywhere, thanks to that Siberian toilet water you like to bathe in so much."

The man drew himself stiffly erect and huffed. "It is French *eau de cologne!*"

"Call it what you will," scoffed Baba Yaga. "It still stinks."

The man the witch addressed as Ivan Ulyanovich Dzhansky looked ready to answer back with something scathing. Then he appeared to reconsider the wisdom of his retort and settled for an irritated shrug as he resumed his trudge along the path to the hut. He stopped a few steps beyond the open gate in the fence.

As one, all of the skulls sitting atop their stakes turned in his direction. Their sockets now glowed with a warm yellow light. Ivan Ulyanovich shuddered at their bony stares.

"I am surprised to still find you living here," he said.

"And where should I be?" answered the witch, with a loud sniff. "In a dacha by the Black Sea, maybe? With former commissars and retired KGB bosses, all of them bloated and rich with corruption, as my neighbours?" Baba Yaga spat. "The thought of seeing those *svinyi* sleeping in the sun on the beach with their fat white asses shoved inside skimpy swimsuits makes even me want to vomit."

Baba Yaga shuddered at the image in her mind. "No, I am where I am supposed to be, and always will be, and want to be."

A sly smile slipped over the witch's face. "Ah, Ivan Ulyanovich Dzhansky, the seasons have not been kind to you, though. I remember a young and clean and eager apparatchik who would come to see me and ask advice on behalf of Brezhnev. Always, of course, for the good of Holy Mother Russia you came." The witch sniggered. "And here you come once more to my little izba, only now you are grown old and fat and slow. Brezhnev is dead, and Russia is not so holy now with the devils who drive her along. It must be desperate times indeed for any to seek aid from me."

"What do you … How do you—?" sputtered Dzhansky, who fell silent when Baba Yaga lifted a finger.

"I know that you know that I am no fool," said the old wise woman. "I can see inside your heart, Ivan Ulyanovich. In my dark mirror I also see all that was, all that is, and all that may be and will be. I see death, I see destruction, and I see all those who push back against your masters. Pushing back very well, I must say, to the misery of the Kremlin."

"These are only temporary setbacks," muttered Ivan, even as Baba Yaga chortled.

"Say you so?" The old witch grinned. "It seems more to me that things do not go quite so well for the bear these days. The eagle's talons claw at his face and the bulldog chews on his leg. I hear that even the beaver bites the bear on the bum. The world builds fences all around the bear, who must now go begging on bended knee to the dragon for help."

Baba Yaga waited, but there was no retort from Dzhansky. She shrugged and spat again at the ground in front of her visitor. "Well, then, what is it you want? Or, should I say, what is it that your *dolboyob* bosses want?"

Dzhansky's eyebrows lifted, wrinkling his bald forehead. "You're in a hurry to know, Grandmother."

Baba Yaga smiled in appreciation at the tardy title of grudging respect. Then she shrugged a narrow shoulder. "Why waste time?" She scoffed. "The sooner you tell me what you want, the sooner I can say no and the sooner you can go."

Dzhansky remained silent for several long moments. "You are ordered — no," the old apparatchik corrected himself, seeing Baba Yaga's raised eyebrow, "*asked* to serve the country as you did in the past and — "

"*Serve?*" interrupted Baba Yaga, glaring at a cringing Dzhansky.

"Help!" the old apparatchik cried as he corrected himself again. "They ask for your help in the struggle to free those who suffer from corrupt politicians and vicious criminals!"

Stone-faced, Baba Yaga listened to the rush of words from the dread-stricken Ivan Ulyanovich Dzhansky. When the other finished, she remained silent for the count of three slow heartbeats. Then her head inclined in a slow nod.

"Is that all, then, my dear old Ivan Ulyanovich?" Baba Yaga asked.

Dzhansky hesitated, taken aback at the sweet tone of the old witch's voice. With hope kindling in his heart, he answered, "Yes, Grandmother, that is all."

"Only that, Ivan Ulyanovich. Only that one thing, and no more?"

"*Da!*" replied Dzhansky, confident now of a successful conclusion to his mission. A vision grew in his mind of receiving an official promotion and, perhaps, an offer of a retirement dacha by the Black Sea.

Baba Yaga smiled. "Нет."

Dzhansky's dream dacha collapsed and vanished. He blinked and stared at Baba Yaga. "*Nyet?* But … no … you can't mean — "

"H. E. T," said Baba Yaga, uttering each letter with obvious pleasure.

"But you can't!" spluttered Dzhansky. "No one says no to them!"

The old witch's thick grey eyebrows lifted. "Say you so?" she murmured, and shrugged. "Well, maybe those *dolboyob* should get used to the word no. The fools will be hearing it often in the days and years to come."

Baba Yaga turned away and began to walk back to her garden. "*Do svidaniya*, Ivan Ulyanovich Dzhansky," she said over a shoulder. "Do not come back."

Behind her she heard a single step and a loud hollow smack, followed by a pained yelp. Baba Yaga smiled, seeing in her mind Dzhansky moving to follow her with more pleading, just as her fence gate swung shut and its bony palings struck him hard across his protruding stomach.

At the edge of her garden, Baba Yaga stopped and turned partway around. She saw the slouched back of a dejected Ivan Ulyanovich Dzhansky dwindling in the distance as he slowly walked down the path to the dark forest and the road to Moscow beyond the horizon.

"Now we will see what happens next," she said, chuckling.

"Unfortunately," murmured the cat, stretched out with eyes closed on the front step of the hut.

A few days later, Baba Yaga was outside her little izba, inspecting the crop of mushrooms and other fungi sprouting all over the rotted tree stumps and logs near a shaded corner of her garden. She crouched down for a better look at several vile-looking toadstools, swiped a hand across each purple head, and then licked the tips of her fingers.

"Mmmm," she murmured. "A little longer, I think, for better flavour. But not bad." She nodded with a satisfied smile. "Not bad."

The clacking of bony teeth sounded behind her. But the chattering of the skulls was almost drowned out by the sudden, grumbling roar of diesel engines.

"Company's coming," murmured the cat from the front step, as it rolled over into a better sleeping position.

Grunting with the effort, Baba Yaga stood up and turned to see what foolish event threatened to interfere with her day.

Four large motor vehicles burst out of the woods beyond her hut. Baba Yaga knew them for armoured troop cars, the kind she saw often now in her dark mirror during evenings when she amused herself by watching the world at war.

The APVs drove fast in a straight line across the clearing. Near the top of the rise, the lead vehicle slowed just long enough for the other three to veer off and bring themselves into formation on either side. They braked a short distance from the fence surrounding Baba Yaga's hut.

The skulls shook so much atop their bony palings that their jaws rattled.

Baba Yaga made a show of hobbling up to the fence. She rested a hand on one skull. It stilled at her touch as did all of its bony brethren. Their eye sockets glowed first white, then yellow, before turning a dark, smouldering red.

Baba Yaga waited on her side of the fence. A door opened on one of the APVs and a man in uniform and a peaked cap stepped out. He stood aside from the door and, after a moment, another man climbed out. A thin smile of recognition crept across Baba Yaga's wrinkled face.

"Ivan Ulyanovich Dzhansky!" she called out. "Back again?" The old witch shook her head. "You don't hear so well, I think. So sad in a man of your age. I recall telling you not to come see me again."

Dzhansky arched his back with a loud crack and shook himself all over before answering. "I heard what you said, Grandmother."

"Then you don't listen — is that the problem?"

Dzhansky swiped a hand across his bald head as he stepped forward, past the front of the APV. "I heard," he said. "I listened."

He stopped two steps away from the fence. He ignored the skulls as they turned in his direction. "I took your refusal back to Moscow. Then I listened to my superiors." He shrugged. "Now I am here again, Baba Yaga, to tell you what my superiors told me."

Baba Yaga lifted an eyebrow. "You fear them more than me?"

Dzhansky glanced over a shoulder at the officer with the leytenánt's insignia on his cap. "I have a better chance," he said in a lowered voice, "of finding *you* in a good mood and willing to let me leave again after I speak, than I have that my superiors would *not* assign me to a new post in Siberia if I refused to see you again."

Baba Yaga chuckled. "Maybe, maybe," she said. "Well, then, Ivan Ulyanovich, what message do you have for me today?"

Dzhansky sighed. "They do not accept your refusal," he said, speaking aloud again as he swept an arm behind him. "These men are here under the command of Leytenánt Laskin to escort you to Moscow."

Baba Yaga regarded the line-up of APVs. "Say you so?" She clicked her tongue. "And if I decline this kind invitation?"

Before Dzhansky could respond, Leytenánt Laskin strode up beside him with a solid stamp of the feet as he snapped to attention. "Enough talk!" he declared, raising a hand to point at Baba Yaga. "You will come with us! That is an order!"

Baba Yaga looked up and down at him then returned her attention to Dzhansky. "The problem with young people these days," she said, gesturing with a thumb at the leytenánt, "is that they have no respect for the old." She sighed. "Not like it once was."

"You will come with us!" ordered the leytenánt, his face growing red. "Now!"

Baba Yaga shook her head. The eye sockets of every skull atop the fence blazed like burning coals. The witch sighed and then smiled. "Well," she said, turning slowly around, "I suppose I should get my little hut in order, then."

Ivan Ulyanovich Dzhansky's face turned white. The witch's cat jumped up from the front step and ran off into the garden. Dzhansky began sidling away from the leytenánt, who only stamped a foot as he told Baba Yaga to hurry. The old witch nodded in response. She took a single step away from the fence and then stopped.

She lifted a hand.

Little hut, little hut, listen and attend close to me now.
Little hut, stretch a leg.
Little hut, shake a leg.
Little hut, little hut, I have work for you to do for me now.

Baba Yaga turned about and returned to the fence. Behind her, the izba suddenly rose up from the ground on a pair of gigantic chicken legs that were as thick as tree trunks. It loomed over Baba Yaga, who grinned now, showing off a full set of gleaming, steel-tipped teeth.

"Tovarisch Dzhansky, what is this?" demanded Leytenánt Laskin as he looked around, expecting to see Dzhansky beside him. Instead he saw Dzhansky's retreating back as the old apparatchik ran past the rearmost of the APVs and down the hillside towards the forest.

The leytenánt shouted an order. Soldiers poured out of the APVs and took up defensive positions.

"You cannot refuse," Leytenánt Laskin started to say, as he turned back to face Baba Yaga. The rest of his arrogant words stuck fast in his throat. He looked up at two great long chicken legs towering above, and on top of them the izba, bending over, its open door like a single great dark eye staring down at him.

Baba Yaga chuckled. "Time for you to go."

The izba stepped forward, its chicken legs carrying it over the fence. It planted itself in front of the lead APV.

The soldiers fell back, bringing their assault rifles up. But before they could shoot, one of the izba's legs lifted and swung back. The leg hung poised for a moment then swung forward. Its scaly four-toed chicken foot slammed against the APV. The izba's kick sent the armoured car flying through the air. It crashed down on the ground behind the other APVs.

"I think you want to leave now."

Leytenánt Laskin turned to see Baba Yaga's steel-tipped grin flashing before his eyes.

"*Da,*" he said, head nodding like a bobblehead doll. He shouted orders even as he started backing away from Baba Yaga.

All of the soldiers began a slow withdrawal from the vicinity of the izba. The hut ignored them, turning instead towards another APV and lifting its leg to kick.

Leytenánt Laskin and his soldiers retreated in proper order past the last APV, then turned and fled down the hill towards the forest. They heard a metallic crash as another armoured car landed on top of the wreck of the first one. They kept on running, the leytenánt glancing back just once to see the izba jumping up and down on the two remaining APVs, flattening them both.

He ran faster then, reaching the edge of the forest just as his men vanished among the trees. He stopped for one last look back. The izba was bouncing one of the crumpled APVs up and down on a scaly chicken-leg knee, as if it were Andriy Shevchenko performing for a cheering crowd in a championship football match.

Baba Yaga waved from behind her bone fence.

"*Do svidanya*," she called.

The witch's shrill laugh rang in the leytenánt's ears all the way back to Moscow.

Baba Yaga lay stretched out on top of the great stone oven in her little izba. The morning baking was done. She enjoyed the lingering warmth from the oven seeping into her old bones. She sighed with contentment and, her long nose twitching and her eyelids closing, was just starting to doze.

Her eyes snapped open at the sound of trees crashing and a grinding roar outside of the hut.

Grunting with the effort, Baba Yaga slid off of the top of the oven, landing on her feet with a thump. She paused to stretch her arms high above her head, with a loud cracking of her joints.

The cat brushed past her legs and headed towards the open doorway of the izba. "They're back," the cat said over one shoulder as it stepped outside and disappeared around the side of the hut.

A short hobble brought the old witch to the doorway. She paused for another joint-popping stretch, then snatched up a decrepit, long-handled broom standing beside the entrance, alongside a big iron pestle and a large iron mortar.

Her head cocked to one side, Baba Yaga listened to the loud and constant *crack-crack-crack!* of trees breaking in the forest beyond her hut.

"More surprise visitors," she muttered. "I am becoming very popular again these days."

Her legs now free of stiffness, Baba Yaga stepped out of the doorway of her hut and looked towards the fence surrounding her yard. The skulls, their eye sockets blazing, bounced up and down with excitement on their bony stakes. The old witch lifted her hawk-sharp eyes and looked beyond the fence.

She saw the pile of flattened armoured cars left behind by the last visitors to her little hut. A brief, amused smile tugged at her lips with the memory, then she looked towards the forest at the edge of the clearing.

Her gaze rested on the edge of the wood just as a monstrous metal machine erupted from the forest, scattering splintered trees left and right before it. To Baba Yaga, who had watched the Soviet and Nazi armies batter each other across the vast frozen Russian steppes and through the densely packed trees of the taiga, this monstrous machine looked something like a tank, only bigger. There was no cannon on the turret of the rolling juggernaut. Instead, beside one of its two top hatches, the barrel of a machine gun pointed towards the sky. A huge arrowhead bulldozer blade, caked with dirt, was mounted on the front of the machine.

"Very nice," said Baba Yaga, admiring the steel-sharp dozer blade. "I could use something like that."

She smiled to herself and made a show of sweeping out some dust from inside the hut as she watched the spectacle setting up outside her little izba.

Moments after the dozer-tank had emerged from the woods, five regular tanks rumbled into view, crawling one by one along the broad pathway ploughed out between the trees. Their clanking treads crushed the stumps left behind by the larger machine. The dozer-tank crawled to a stop a short distance up the slope of the clearing. The five tanks rolled into place in a line behind.

Baba Yaga watched all of this as she continued to sweep. When the last tank had rolled to a rocking stop, the old witch shouldered her broom and pretended to hobble slowly to the open gate in her fence. The skulls on the fence stakes stopped their bouncing and sat still, jaws clacking shut. A dark red light smouldered deep within every eye socket.

On the dozer-tank, the hatch with the machine gun next to it popped open, falling back onto the turret with a *clank*. A man rose out of the hatch. He held a small megaphone in one hand. His officer's cap bore the insignia of a senior lieutenant.

Baba Yaga studied his face and shrugged. A stranger to her. Her long nose twitched, though. It smelled something — someone — familiar amid the stink of diesel fumes.

Resting her sharp chin on her broomstick, Baba Yaga waited and watched.

She didn't wait long. The other hatch fell open with a *clang!* Someone that the old witch knew very well pushed himself up through the narrow opening. Baba Yaga smiled at the sight of the rumpled overcoat and the familiar bald head shining with sweat.

"Ho! Ivan Ulyanovich Dzhansky!" called out Baba Yaga, feigning surprise. "Here you are again? You have brought more of your friends with you too, I see. Now, should I be asking why you have invited yourself to my little hut once more?"

She watched with her sharp eyes as Dzhansky pushed himself up through the tight-fitting hatch as far as his thick waist would allow. She heard with her keen ears the old apparatchik grunt and sigh in frustration. He stretched out an arm and took hold of the little megaphone that the tank commander handed him.

"Baba Yaga," he said into the megaphone. "I am here to tell you that you are now *ordered* to come to Moscow." His free arm waved at the five tanks lined up behind him. "They are here to escort you there."

Baba Yaga tsked loudly. "Is it so?" she said. On either side of her, all along the fence, the eye sockets of every skull turned black as the midnight sky. "Well," she said, with a shrug of her bony shoulders, "if this is what the fools want, then let it be so."

She turned about and hobbled back towards the hut. "Let me just get some things packed," she called over a shoulder, "and we will be on our way."

Baba Yaga vanished into the hut. The stárshiy leytenánt smirked as he watched her disappear through the doorway. "Not so difficult," he said, turning towards Dzhansky. "From what I was told, I had expected—"

What the stárshiy leytenánt expected, he never said. His mouth shut at the sight of the old apparatchik struggling again to pull himself out through the dozer-tank hatch. Dzhansky grunted and swore as he twisted and pushed against the top of the turret—all in vain, it seemed, as his wide waist refused to shift even a single millimetre more.

Old fool, the tank commander thought with a mental sneer, as he turned forward again. He gaped at the sight of Baba Yaga's little izba rising up on its great scaly legs. From within the dark doorway of the hut, there sounded a loud metallic ringing like the striking of a huge gong.

Out of the izba, banging and clanging, shot Baba Yaga, sitting in her great iron mortar and beating the side of it with the long iron pestle. She soared above the collection of mechanized armour gathered outside of her hut. The heads of the tank commander and Dzhansky turned to follow her path through the air. Dzhansky then returned his attention to trying to force his overweight body out through the hatch.

The stárshiy leytenánt ignored the old apparatchik's struggles as he watched the witch turn her great iron mortar about in the air and send it, banging and clanging, down towards the row of tanks. The hatches on the turrets remained closed, but the stárshiy leytenánt guessed that the tank leader on the far right was giving orders to his crew, for the turret of that one swivelled to its left and the barrel of its cannon slowly rose.

Too late, though. The iron mortar turned on its side, with Baba Yaga holding onto the rim with her left hand as her right swung the iron pestle.

Bang! The pestle struck the barrel of the tank. The barrel bent sideways. "Ho ho!" laughed Baba Yaga in her screechy voice. The iron mortar sailed straight up above the tanks, turned a cartwheel in the air, and dove down again, with Baba Yaga waving her iron pestle.

"Ha ha!" she cried, striking the cannon barrel of the next tank with a loud *bang*, leaving the end of it pointing down to the ground. "Hee hee!" laughed the old witch, as she flew up again and then dove towards the next tank.

Bang! Bang! Bang! Up and down and round and round flew Baba Yaga in her iron mortar, leaving in her wake bent cannon barrels pointing in every direction but straight.

The stárshiy leytenánt cursed and shook a fist in the air as he turned in his hatch to watch Baba Yaga flying about. Then he yelped and ducked down fast, just in time to see the scaly bottoms of the little izba's huge chicken feet as they sailed over the dozer-tank.

The stárshiy leytenánt heard a loud metallic *thunk* followed by muffled yelling. He rose slowly up in his hatch to look behind the dozer-tank. Baba Yaga's hut was dancing back and forth along the line of tanks, skipping from one metal turret to another. Each of them slowly bent and buckled under the repeated blows of the big chicken feet as the hut danced from one end of the line of tanks to the other, over and over. From inside the machines came the muted screams of the trapped crews, now crowded within the space beneath each crumpled turret.

"Ha ha, hee hee, ho ho!" cried Baba Yaga, waving her pestle towards the izba. "Your fun is all done, now away you go."

The hut stopped dancing. It turned first one way then the other, then it jumped up and down one last time on each of the five tanks. The little izba hopped off of the last tank and leaped over the dozer-tank. It skipped up the hill, jumped over the bone fence, and, with a final turnabout so that its doorway faced towards the woods, folded its legs and settled back down on the ground.

The stárshiy leytenánt ducked inside his tank again and watched through the hatch opening as the izba passed over him. With relief, he poked his head out of the hatch just in time to bang his skull hard on the bottom of Baba Yaga's iron mortar. Stunned, he tumbled back into the machine's cramped interior as the daylight through the hatch vanished.

Baba Yaga landed her mortar on the dozer-tank. It settled on top of the open hatch beside Dzhansky. The machine gun beside the hatch collapsed with a screech under the crushing weight of the mortar.

"That was fun," said the witch, with a smile on her hatchet-like face. "Now, Ivan Ulyanovich, it is time for us to go, you and I."

Dzhansky had ceased trying to pull himself out of the dozer-tank's second hatch. Resting his forearms on top of the turret, he slumped forward, head bowed. He glanced over with resignation at Baba Yaga. "And where, Grandmother, are we going to go?"

Baba Yaga chuckled, low and deep. "Why, to Moscow, my child."

Dzhansky sighed. He knew the answer, but he asked the question anyway. "And why *now* are we going to Moscow?"

Baba Yaga looked at him with a smile everywhere on her face except in her eyes. Dzhansky shivered under that cold stare.

"To see the fools who think to summon me, of course. It has been a very long time since anyone courted me with such persistence." Baba Yaga's smile grew wide and her eyes glinted with malice. Dzhansky shuddered in response. "Well, *now* they have my attention, and I think it only right and proper that I answer their demands in such a way that they understand at last what I say. Baba Yaga is not a serf that anyone can command."

With an abrupt turn, Baba Yaga banged her iron pestle against the turret of the dozer-tank. Then she held the pestle over her shoulder so that it pointed towards the line of crumpled tanks behind her.

"Now up, one and all, and on to Moscow we shall go." she commanded.

There was a shuddering and a shaking and then slowly, slowly, all of the tanks lifted up from the ground. As they rose, Baba Yaga waved the pestle in the air and pointed it at the pile of wrecked APVs.

"You too," she ordered.

The flattened armoured cars shivered and then separated, each one rising into the air. Baba Yaga cackled and gestured with her pestle. Obediently, the APVs lined up single file as they rose, as did the five tanks, with the dozer-tank in the lead position.

"Hi ho and away we go!" cried Baba Yaga.

The line of ruined vehicles sailed over the forest in the direction of Moscow.

The cat, sitting in the open doorway of Baba Yaga's little hut, waved goodbye with a paw, then turned about and disappeared inside.

A squad of soldiers marched in the shadow of the Kremlin across the granite paving blocks of Krasnaya Ploshchad. Tourists took photographs. Someone pointed up at the sky.

Tourists and soldiers rubbed stinging eyes as they saw a line of battered tanks and APVs dropping down out of the glaring sun.

Atop the largest hulk, an old woman stood in a great metal bowl, banging it with a large metal paddle. She shrieked with laughter and waved her paddle like a conductor's baton.

Baba Yaga's iron pestle pointed downwards. Stuck in his turret, Dzhansky closed his eyes tight as the dozer-tank dove, its train of wrecked vehicles following behind.

"Hi ho! Hi ho! Hello! Hello!" cried Baba Yaga, waving to the crowd as she, the tanks, and the APVs circled nine times around the nine onion-domed towers of St Basil's Cathedral. With each pass, the dozer-tank brushed against a dome, leaving a scar and spraying down paint and gilt.

"Ho ho! Hee hee! Naughty, naughty," guffawed Baba Yaga, spying the soldiers raising their rifles. Before they could aim, they ducked as the battered tanks and APVs swooped low overhead.

Baba Yaga banged her pestle against the dozer-tank. The metal hulk flew towards the green spires of Spasskaya tower, its fellow wrecks following behind.

"Hi ho! Hee hee! Now look at me," she commanded, waving at the shocked bureaucrats and politicians crowding the windows.

The witch banged her pestle nine times against the dozer-tank. "Hear me now, for our journey is done. Now we'll have a last bit of fun."

The five wrecked tanks separated. They rose above the Kremlin, then reversed. Shattered steel fronts and bent cannons pointed towards the square. They hovered a moment, then plunged down. Four smashed in between granite paving blocks like steel pillars. Muffled cries and curses came from the tank crews trapped inside.

The fifth tank pulled itself horizontal and landed with a hollow *boom* atop the rear of the tank at the far left, creating a giant metal T.

"Good, good," smiled Baba Yaga. "Wait there for your cousins to join you."

The four APVs dropped down towards the tank pillars. One wedged into place like a horizontal bar between two tanks on the right.

Three APVs attached themselves to the single solitary tank. One embedded itself into the granite at the foot of the steel pillar, another slammed against the middle of the tank, and the last fastened itself below the top. The combined wrecks spelled out the letters H E T.

Baba Yaga nodded approval. "Very nice. *Nyet* indeed. Now for you, my wonderful great steed."

She laughed, and Dzhansky yelped in surprise. The dozer-tank somersaulted, then dove down to the square and stopped, its blade tip just touching the unbroken paving stones beside the towering steel T.

"In you go, nice and slow," commanded Baba Yaga.

Steel screeched against stone as the blade pressed down, grinding its sharp tip into the granite. Half the length of the blade pierced the stone, digging deep into the ground before stopping. A mound of earth and stone dust surrounded the blade, like the period of an exclamation mark.

"Fine, fine," Baba Yaga nodded. She sat at ease, not minding that both she and her iron mortar hung at right angles to the ground. Weak banging against the bottom of the mortar came from inside the dozer-tank. The old witch grinned.

"Now, then. One last thing to do before we take our leave," she said.

Baba Yaga banged her pestle against the mortar. It flew off from the dozer-tank and circled around the steel pillars of the wrecked tanks. As she passed, Baba Yaga used her pestle to punch holes in the sides of each of the four upright metal hulks. The fifth tank, sitting atop its fellow wreck, received holes in what remained of its flattened turret.

"Never say that Baba Yaga is unkind," declared the witch to the cursing tank crews inside. "A gift of sweet air for you until someone lets you out."

The stárshiy leytenánt scrambled from the now-open hatch of the dozer-tank. *Not so arrogant now*, Baba Yaga noted with amusement. His crew followed, landing with grunts and groans onto the paving stone. They hobbled off, looking behind in fear of seeing Baba Yaga in pursuit.

The witch circled around the steel monument, waving her pestle. "Hold fast now, all of you."

The mortar stopped beside the dozer-tank. Baba Yaga tapped lightly on the shoulder of Ivan Ulyanovich Dzhansky. The old apparatchik opened his eyes. The first thing he saw, flashing in the sunlight, was Baba Yaga's steely grin.

"So now, my dear old Ivan Ulyanovich, I take my leave of you," she said. "Our last goodbye." He winced as her pestle tapped his shoulder again. "*Never* come to my little izba again. For *any* reason. Retire from service, if you can, or spend your days in Siberia, if you must. But do not let me see you at my gate again."

Baba Yaga laughed at Dzhansky's downcast face. "Yes, I know, you still must make one last report. I wish you whatever luck you find with that."

Baba Yaga pointed at her monument. "There is my answer, the same as when first you showed up at my hut with demands from fools. *Nyet.* If *they* still insist on my help, then they can come themselves to my little izba, and hear me say *nyet* to their faces."

The old witch chuckled. "Better still, if they even think about sending someone else, or dare to come themselves, to my little hut in the woods, they should look out the window first and save themselves the trouble — and me the bother."

Baba Yaga winked and patted Dzhansky's cheek. "They may not like to hear *nyet*, but fools should get used to hearing others say no."

Cackling loudly, Baba Yaga struck her pestle against the mortar. It spun round and rose up. Once around the Kremlin it flew, then it shot away into the sky, disappearing over the horizon.

Did anything of what I said actually happen? Who knows? In the Kremlin they talk about 'propaganda and lies', but they do so far from any window looking out upon Red Square.

That is all I can say, so I will say no more.

Go ask the cat if you don't believe me.

RAGNABEÐTÍMI: BEDTIME OF THE GODS

DA Cooper

DA Cooper is a poet from Texas. His work has recently appeared in Autumn Sky Poetry DAILY, Dialogue Journal, Light, Lighten Up Online, New Verse Review, The Road Not Taken, and Witcraft, among others. He enjoys translating dialect poetry from Italy, watching The Office, and looking at trees.

Ragnabeðtími:
Bedtime of the Gods

The little Æsir children rally all
Valhalla to the final valorous battle.
They stand against the ancient, fearsome giants
with boldness, fighting bravely, yet they know
their struggle is in vain; defeat assured—
their fates have been foretold, bedtime has come.

The great wolf's howls chill wise Alltoddler's heart.
Despite his dread, brave Odin fights, resists
with valor, leads his warriors to the fray.
He charges forth yet knows that all is lost.
With massive, monstrous paws, vast Flossrir grabs
the little godling's face and cleans his teeth.

The thunder maker knows no fear, defies
the mighty, loathsome wyrm, Pajamagandr.
The sleepwear serpent seeks to snatch the godling,
catch him in great cloth coils. Their fight is fierce.

It seems that Thor has triumphed, but the snake
brings down the burly brawler in the end.

The sleepy giant wields his flaming sword
and flings its calming warmth at mighty Freyr.
Great Snooztr and the Vanr, bold and brave,
fight on until the Nine Worlds are ablaze.
An ashen dimness follows, and all yield
unto the coming sleep, Ragnabeðtími.

The gloom of Fimbulslumber enters bones
and muscles as the candle of the heavens
sinks down; the sky's black blanket covers all
of Asgard, Midgard, and the other realms.
The end comes in a cold and soundless whimper
as deepening twilight spreads across the land.

HOW TO WRITE A NOVEL IN TEN DAYS DURING THE ZOMBIE APOCALYPSE

Jakob Drud

Jakob lives in Aarhus, Denmark, with his girlfriend and children. He's been writing science fiction and fantasy for the past twenty years and loves fiction that surprises, brings new insights, and makes him laugh. He's published more than forty short stories in English, and in Danish he's the author of a two-book series called The Shadow Lens. You can find his story 'Culinary Subjugation' in Pulp Literature Issue 27, Summer 2020.

Z

How to Write a Novel in Ten Days During the Zombie Apocalypse

Day 1

Some of you may have seen the name Hogan W Perdue in huge letters on the cover of a bestseller, back in the days before the Big Z. Fifty novels in print and coast-to-coast book tours. Science fiction, crime, pirate adventure, romance, and rose gardening. Hogan's done it all.

But lately I've been slacking. I mean, it's easy to come up with excuses for not writing in the face of the Big Z. I was abroad when it happened, the book market's gone through the floor, and half my potential readers are shambling through the streets looking for brains. The only things on people's reading lists are the best-before dates on canned goods. Excuses? I got excuses.

Except yesterday I had an epiphany.

I was out with Ajax, Bolstoj, and Ajax's teenage daughter, Pennyblossom, scavenging a farmhouse three miles from the holiday resort we've turned into a fenced compound. We were ambushed by five Zs, probably the former inhabitants, and a glorious gorefest-slash-screaming session ensued. Kinda like the job I did as a bouncer in my pre-Z youth. But then this weird thing happened: Pennyblossom took her bow and tip-toed upstairs, where she started flipping through the picture books belonging to the farmer's kids. And I saw that girl smiling, even though she'd just shot them kids downstairs in the kitchen!

That's when it came to me: the world needs an escape from the misery of post-Z society. So I'm gonna write something with dragons and unicorns and giants and sorcerers in it. Something where the heroes survive their trials instead of getting cornered and eaten by their rotting neighbours.

No day for it like today, and I'm off to a flying start. At first light I sat down at the trusty Remington typewriter I found at the antique shop and put in six pages. I took a break to relieve Jomilla on perimeter duty at ten, then back to it after a quick can of beans. Another seven pages before I had to muck out the barn and empty the slush bucket from the john (a chore my main character, Jake, farmboy turned hero, tries hard to escape). Another six pages got done before I had to leave the compound to gather firewood with Gore, Ajax, and the Pole.

Aiming to get three or four more pages in before I pull the first night shift. Hopefully, it'll be dull, giving me enough time to figure out what Jake packs for his dragon hunt. I wonder what chance encounters are gonna turn him aside from his quest. Perhaps he meets a starving artist? An axe-wielding barbarian and his daughter-gone-wild? Except that sounds too much like life around these parts. I'll have to come up with something a little more glorious. Perhaps I'll even add a character who owns a bar of soap.

I'll keep this journal going for posterity. In the old days, it was a good tool to keep myself accountable, and besides, what else can I do on my breaks when Snapchat is down?

Day 2

Making good time. Started out with twenty-three pages yesterday and doubled that today. Typewriter's smokin' hot, I tell you, and the story's a blast. 'Course, I'm privileged to live in a walled community with twenty-four-hour guards, but really, any writer worth their salt could do this.

That got me thinking back to the days before civilization fell apart. Over the years, I've heard writers complain that it takes them ages to write a short story, let alone something as monstrous as a novel. They state as an absolute fact that writing must be slow or else the quality will suffer. Well, they couldn't be more wrong. Just type that thing up, keep the plot going, and don't skimp on the action.

Ajax brought back a rumour that someone with a working drone caught sight of large swarms of Zs hiking out of Berlin. The worst of it'll hit our community in about two weeks, so I'd better be done by then, since we'll likely have to run. And there's no way I'm hauling this old typewriter through the wilderness. You need the other kind of Remington for a trip like that — plus ammo, which we're short on.

So, twenty-three pages done, and the only chore I had to skip was today's longbow practice with Pennyblossom. Not a big loss, though, since I'll probably get some shots in during guard duty tonight. Ajax didn't hear wrong; there really do seem to be more Zs around.

Day 3

Ajax came back today with a scratch on his face. Not as bad as a bite, and Astral says he did good pouring whisky on it. Me, I'm kinda suspicious he really did it. I mean, the Ajax I know would have drunk the whisky and been done with it, but it could be he poured it on his face and caught the runoff with his mouth. Anyway, I'll keep an eye on him for the next day or so. Don't want him Z'ing out on us in our sleep.

I didn't tell you about Astral, did I? Sweet lady, mid-forties, meditation, veggie diet, used to visit cloisters in Tibet. You think you know her kind, but no. She's a chemist turned investment banker and absolutely fabulous with a hatchet at close range, but mostly she fills the role of community doctor. She says that if Ajax's wounds start to heal up in the next day or so, he won't get the Z infection. Pennyblossom gave him a kick for not looking out for himself, so I guess she's optimistic too.

All that infectious scratching business gave me the idea for Jake's next companion. Now, Jake thinks Bianca is just another tavern wench, while in fact she's really Princess Cornucopia of the High Kingdom. She's in hiding, and she has a dark secret: recently she was bitten by a magical rainbow, and now every time the sun shines through the rain, she turns into a horned horse. Yes, dear reader, we've got ourselves a wereunicorn! And that's another twenty-two pages completed, including their daring ride into a drizzly sunset to escape the King's men.

Day 4

Started very early because I couldn't sleep. I'm fifty-three, and though the pressure of building a career lessened remarkably when most of the reviewers turned into walking corpses—no big change there, now that I think of it—I'm still wondering if I should be spending my time differently. Like, I don't know, digging more pits outside the chain-link fence or finding a cure for the Z plague.

Being neither doctor nor ditch-digger, I decided to spend my awake time at the typewriter, so I got twelve pages done before I had to stir the fire to make morning stew for the crew. Summary: Jake and Princess Cornucopia meet Whineton. He's a mime, and by using signs and gestures, he manages to negotiate passage for them through The Land of the Clan of Named Centaurs. The centaurs are still suspicious of the wereunicorn princess, though, so trouble's brewing, just the way I like it.

Good thing I had an early start, too, because Astral went and blew herself up. Remember I said she was a chemist? We'd taken a vote and told her to stay away from explosives, what with her getting shaking fits from her PTSD and all, but she must have started fiddling with pipe bombs again after Ajax got scratched. What can I say? Community regulations and common sense never sat well with Astral. (She must have been one hell of an investment banker.)

We're down one shed and one doctor, but at least we don't have to worry about her coming back to eat us. Usually, people start twitching right after they die, but Astral sure put herself to rest. Leastways, there's no life in any of the pieces of her we found. I guess all that meditation really does give a person peace.

Ajax was doing fine up to that point, facial scars healing nicely. Trouble is, the poor bugger was sleeping next door to Astral's shed, so he's a little worse for wear after his place caved in. There's a big lump on his head where a roof pane hit him, and a ten-inch splinter through his right thigh. We got it out, but the wound's on the nasty side of horrible. Didn't help that he's a bit of a wuss and wouldn't lie still while me and the Pole stitched him up, so it's gonna be one hell of a scar. Also, Pennyblossom didn't kick him today, so I guess we're officially worried.

Day 5

Typical. I'm running out of ribbon for the typewriter. I didn't see this coming, and I definitely thought I had another one in a tin can somewhere, but I can't seem to find it. Didn't help that Pennyblossom threw a teenage tantrum in my room earlier, tossing the place. Something about my generation laying waste to her world with the global warming that led to the Z-pocalypse or something. Made me kinda miss the old internet conspiracies where all we had to worry about were chemtrails and the Earth being flat. Now we have stories about the Zs from Berlin getting closer, and that doesn't sound like fake news to me.

I'll try to re-blacken the old ribbon with some fabric dye I scavenged from a thrift store. It's funny what people leave behind these days. Used to be hot among middle-class wannabe thrifters to update old clothes, but now that thrifting's for real, everyone just goes for the canned dog food. I don't know which is less civilized.

Since I've no idea how far the dye'll get me, I'm gonna cut back on the plot to save pages. Slaughtered the Named Centaurs prematurely in a battle today, and Whineton the mime needed to shut up, so I let the dragon have him. Book's actually turning out better for these real-world trip-ups, so despite everything, I'm in an okay mood. Guess I'm gonna forgive Pennyblossom for tossing the room. Besides, with Ajax's wound still looking nasty, someone needs to cut her some slack. I just didn't think it'd have to be me.

Day 6

It was a slow day until 12:44, when it suddenly wasn't. Pennyblossom barged into my room while I was navigating Jake through a dark dungeon to find the Ultimate Dragonslayer. (This plot prop is an unexpected problem. I've changed it from a poisonous sheep to a magical lasso to the Blade of Infinite Doom. It's now a butter knife, only magical, and good luck to Jake stabbing the dragon with that one.)

Anyway, at 12:44, Pennyblossom effectively took my brain out of commission for the day. She just stood in the doorway, arms folded across her chest, and looked at me until I turned away from the typewriter. Then she said, "I'm gonna need a new dad."

I never had a family, so I couldn't tell if this was normal behaviour in a fourteen-year-old or if it's just a sign of the end of the world.

"I'm kinda busy," I said.

"How very dadlike," she answered.

She took out a lighter, and I had to guard my manuscript with my life until I caught onto what she was really trying to say. So now I'm calling it a day to get Bolstoj and the Pole together for an expedition to find some antibiotics for Ajax. Easier said than done, that. We're short on unlooted pharmacies around these parts, and the supermarkets never carried antibiotics. Maybe a nearby drug store has something lying about. I doubt it, but we'll go look.

$\mathcal{D}$AY 7

Well, the world is officially a deadlier place. No more antibiotics anywhere. Not that the overuse of antibiotics in the old world wouldn't eventually have led to lethal, multi-resistant bacterial strains, but today was the dividing line for me: the definitive loss of something I used to take for granted.

The only halfway useful thing I found on the expedition was a handful of belladonna berries. Jake tries to cure Princess Cornucopia of her wereunicorn condition with *Belladonna Atropa*, but I seem to recall something about them being poisonous as well as medicinal. So now I miss Wikipedia too.

Upside: smacking Zs into shelves of dietary supplements with a shopping basket is hilarious, so the expedition wasn't a complete failure. Downside: there were a lot more Zs around than usual, and there really is such a thing as too much fun.

Pennyblossom took it all in stride. "He's my fourth daddy, you know," she said. "'Bout time I had another." But she did sit with Ajax for the entire day, which I gather is Most Unusual for a fourteen-year-old.

I admit I took refuge in the novel after that. Thirty pages in total (couldn't sleep anyway). Jake didn't cure Princess Cornucopia, but I got a dragon attack in before Jake and the princess ruined the book with too much accept-who-you-really-are drivel. Left them holed up in a ruined castle, but it's obvious they'll have to come out and fight the dragon any day now.

Day 8

Weather's been terrible. Rains so strong I figure even the Zs wanted to stay inside, or maybe they got stuck in the mud somewhere. If we're lucky, it'll flash-dry and fix them in place permanently. Remember that game, Plants vs. Zombies? No one's been doing any weeding around these parts for the past three years, and we've got creeper vines up to our ears, so we can hope, right?

Right. They're coming, and no rainy day's gonna change that.

Downpour continued from dusk till dawn, so no going out except to milk the cow, and a lot of words got pounded out on the typewriter. The 'e' has come unhinged, and I have to fill it in by hand, but I hear that's to be expected toward the end of a crazy project. I just keep typing, stopping only to empty the bucket under the hole in the roof. I'm so close to the end now I can smell it. It's a sweet, perfumed scent, like Astral's incense. If only Ajax's wounds smelled half as sweet, but I don't know what's more rotten: his wound or his luck.

Day 9

Just six thousand more words tomorrow and I'll be ready to turn the story in. Three sessions today and another three tomorrow, and we're ready.

Being this close to the end started me thinking about which publishing house I'll use. With my mind in overdrive I forgot to stake two of the pits we dug yesterday. Bad Hogan. *Bad!* I've got to keep it real. We don't have any wereunicorns around to spear the Zs for us, although we could really use some right about now.

Before the Big Z, I wouldn't have given the publishing world much thought, but it's safe to say that the business has changed with the times. Gone are the days of brick-and-mortar stores and libraries. Now you've got to get your book onto the right trading coaches in order to reach an audience. Distribution, people—distribution's where it's at. And in case you're stuck in the old ways: self-publication is no longer an option. Not unless you've got your own caravan and a shitload of ammo.

I've considered asking the people over at Thor's Forge. They are close by, holed up in an old ironworks just three hours away on bicycle. They've got hammers and other mêlée weapons to help distribution. (And they call on some old deity for power. Whatever.) But they're also really big on the Oxford comma, and I'm *not* gonna retype an entire novel on an unravelling ribbon just to keep some bearded editor dude happy. Especially since the copy-editing will probably be done in a mead stupor.

Most of the other publishers are several weeks' travel away, so I guess I'll go with the only other real option around these parts: the Amazons. No one gets a book through the droves of Zs like a bunch of expert archer-warrior women. I'm not too keen, mind you; they're fiercely greedy employers if what I hear is right—I mean, how many people can live on food stamps these days? But when we run from the Berlin Zs we'll be heading in their direction, so I'm basically happy if they'll take us in. Even if they don't take me on a book tour, a safe place to stay looks like a pretty good perk right now.

Day 10

Packing it up. Bolstoj came back from his watch at the church tower a few minutes ago and said about a thousand Zs will hit us around midnight. We may be safe behind the fence for a while, but we'll need to go out for forage eventually, and there's no way we can do that with a bunch of brain-fans blocking our doorstep. So we're running. I've got my longbow and arrows, beef jerky, what's left of Astral's marmalade, a stack of flatbread, two gallons of water, and a change of clothes.

Aaaand I'm bringing one manuscript of fantastic awesomeness, only slightly truncated because Bolstoj called the evacuation earlier than expected. Had to shorten Jake's eulogy for his mentor to three pages, but it's probably for the best. It's kinda hard to teach anyone to dwell on the beauty of a life well lived when today's memorial services are basically a fight over the deceased's toothbrush.

I'll be sad to leave the compound. It's been my safe haven for six months, and I really came to like having a roof over my head, but there'll be no coming back. We've dug enough spiked pits to trap a hundred Zs, and in addition, we're gonna open the gate. We rigged a row of firebombs that'll torch the place, and that should be enough to take a lot of Zs out of the game and keep the rest off our tail.

I just hope we'll be out of sight when it happens, because Ajax volunteered to stay behind and trigger the bomb. To see the place go up like that and know he's in there? His real-life heroics will have me running and crying at the same time.

This is the end of my diary. Right now, Pennyblossom's stringing her bow and yelling at me to finish up, and since I promised Ajax I'd look after her, I guess she's family. That comes with obligations, apparently, such as not letting the wee one get eaten, but there are perks too. Like Pennyblossom handing over the typewriter ribbon she swiped from my room. So, yeah, I've got a family now. A dysfunctional one, maybe, but these days I guess you take what you can find.

*A*FTERWORD

They turned it down. The bloody Amazons turned my novel down, and I'm devastated.

Do you have any idea what it's like to write? You have all kinds of expectations about what it's gonna be like to finally get your story out there in the world (such as it is). You dream of making the rounds to the safe communities, riding the editor's best coach, guards at your side puncturing Z skulls left and right so you aren't spattered with gore when you meet your readers. I'd like to try that, just once. But it's not to be.

Two good things, though. They hired Pennyblossom for their elite archer corps the moment they saw her shoot. My baby girl's gonna go places! And they agreed to publish this diary. Editor said it was a bit short, but she called it 'a slice of life', 'a perfect documentation of the state of the world', and 'slightly less hackneyed than that stupid novel'. Me being a sucker for praise, I accepted on the spot.

I did ask her why they turned down the novel and got a chilling answer.

"People don't want no stinking unicorns," she said. "Readers want social realism that reveals the chains that bind us in this world, and they want to see their heroes cut those chains and make the world a better place."

Social realism?! I guess it's time to face the fact that we've come to the end of the world.

THE HUMMINGBIRD FLASH FICTION PRIZE

THE 2024 HUMMINGBIRD FLASH FICTION PRIZE

The Hummingbirds that flitted into our inbox this year were small but mighty, delicate but piercing. We didn't envy our esteemed judge, Finnian Burnett, who had the task of choosing between them. They had this to say about the winner and honourable mentions:

Winner: **Cheryl Skory Suma, 'The Art of Tear Eating and Other Non-predatory Behaviours'**
"I loved the juxtaposition of scientific facts about butterflies with the painful reality of life with another human whose shared traumas don't always align in peace and love. The story's throughline felt poignant, and the interspersed musings about tear eating as both a metaphor and an actual plot point were unique and stunning."

Honourable Mentions: **Adam Fout, 'Blue Wax Paper'; and Soramimi Hanarejima, 'Life After Bifurcation'**
"Two wildly different stories—both brilliant and engaging from start to finish. I loved the unusual format of 'Life After Bifurcation' and the slow reveal of the twist in the main characters' friendship. In 'Blue Wax Paper', the author used visceral imagery and emotional interiority to drive home the main character's feeling of absolute uselessness. Both the stories left me thinking about them after first, second, and third readings."

Our heartiest thanks to Finnian Burnett for judging these estimable stories, and to all the authors who feathered the *Pulp Lit* nest with their entries.

The 2024 Hummingbird shortlist:

Adam Fout, 'Blue Wax Paper'
Ciara Gordon, '404 Page Not Found.'
Soramimi Hanarejima, 'Life After Bifurcation'
Melanie Mayer, 'Late Night Conversations with the Monster Under the Bed'
Pattie Palmer-Baker, '2020 Circus'
Pattie Palmer-Baker, 'A Star Not a Skeleton'
Kevin Sandefur, 'Flotsam'
Cheryl Skory Suma, 'The Art of Tear Eating and Other Non-predatory Behaviours'
Margot Spronk, 'Out the Window'
KT Wagner, 'Red Corner on Forgotten Street'

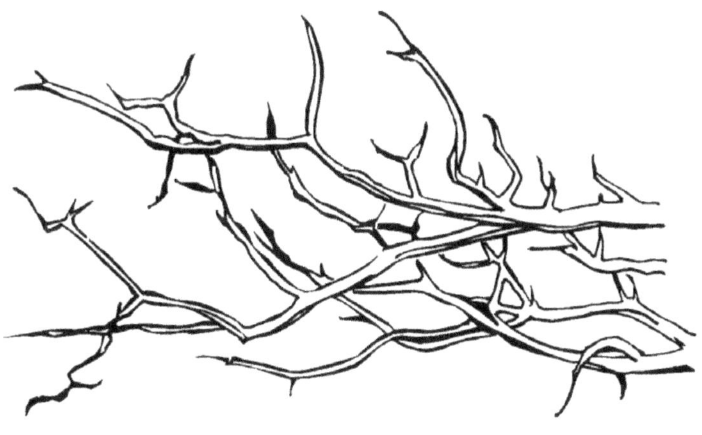

Cheryl Skory Suma's fiction, creative non-fiction, poetry, and photography have appeared in US, UK, and Canadian publications, including Barren Magazine, *the* Aesthetica Creative Writing Award Anthology, Exposition Review, Blank Spaces Magazine, Reckon Review, *and many others. A multi-Pushcart nominee, her work has placed in fifty-one competitions since* 2019. *Cheryl's a past CNF contributing editor at* Barren Magazine. *Her story 'Adrift off the Shore of Alzheimer Island' was runner-up for the* 2022 Bumblebee Flash Fiction Contest, *and you can read it in* Pulp Literature Issue 37, Autumn 2022. *You can find Cheryl on Twitter/X and BlueSkySocial* @cherylskorysuma

The Art of Tear Eating and Other Non-predatory Behaviours

By Cheryl Skory Suma

Yesterday, as I was exiting the parking garage to our apartment, I saw a butterfly. She was beating her wings against the soiled sidewall window, so close to freedom and yet with no hope of escape. If only she would follow me down the stairs to the exit, I could hold the door open and set her free. Sadly, she was ensnared in a habituated cycle, drawn to the light just beyond the glass, a light she'd never reach if she stayed on her current course.

Like the butterfly, rather than flying freely through the door just out of reach, I've chosen to thrust against the window before me, focusing outward when really I'm mesmerized by an inward pull. I wish I knew how to find the exit, how to escape this place where we've trapped ourselves.

Unlike birds, butterflies do not flap their wings. Instead, they pull their bodies inward, contracting themselves. This causes air to be forced upward and under their wings, pushing them forward.

I hear you breaking again, your sobs breaching the thin walls of our apartment. I enter the bedroom and crawl silently onto the bed with you, folding my body until it mirrors yours, enveloping you. Two becoming one, cocooned together in a foetal position. When I lift my head to kiss your neck, your tears bridge our cheeks, finding their way to my upper lip. I taste your pain and wonder how I could consume more of you.

Butterflies in the Amazon consume the tears of turtles. Not out of compassion, of course, but rather out of necessity. It offers more than a drink — a quick fix of sodium. This is critical for egg production, for their metabolism. For flight.

When we first met, our shared scars offered salvation, a special bond leading to happier days. Two broken souls trying to cobble themselves together into something functional. For a short while, we succeeded. Yet somehow, neither of us truly escaped our taste for it, our thirst for the moment of grief's release. Kindred in our destructive ways, we eagerly embraced disintegration, believing it essential to our survival.

Without realizing it, we were feeding on one another.

Lachryphagy = the act of crawling into the eyes of another to sip their tears, or 'tear eating'. From the Latin (lacrima = tear) and Greek (phagos = one that eats). It sounds more predatory than it should. The consumption of tears is, after all, strictly for survival.

When your tears end, so does our embrace. You struggle to sit up, to extradite yourself from my support. Without speaking, you pull on your boots and fly out the door.

Butterflies' wings are much larger than required to support their body mass for flight. Even when half of their wings are missing or damaged, they can still fly.

My better half now damaged and flown, I resist the urge to soar out after you. I know you'll return when you're ready. Sadly, we have become accustomed to beating ourselves against this particular window, this narrow view of a life we could leave behind if only the glass would open and set us free.

Unexpectedly, my own tears begin to flow. Once again, I'm mimicking you. I realize I'm famished. Entering the kitchen to start dinner, I stick out my tongue to capture my tears rather than wiping them away.

Something to tide me over until you return.

Adam Fout has work in Pulp Literature, Flash Fiction Online, December, and more. He is a graduate of the 2020 Odyssey Writing Workshop and a professor of technical communication at the University of North Texas. You can find his story 'Black Glass' in Issue 24, Autumn 2019.

BLUE WAX PAPER

BY ADAM FOUT

We sit on aluminum picnic benches, their bases drilled into concrete, the metal shining from the long fluorescent lights in the white ceiling above. I'm wearing the turquoise paper outfit they gave me at check-in, like a pear dressed in blue wax paper. The girl across from me wears a brown full-body jumpsuit with a teddy bear hood, the hair on its little ears fluttering in the air conditioning that's making me shiver so hard my teeth chatter. Someone brought her clothes.

I don't have anyone to bring me clothes.

She crunches on an apple.

"So," she says, mouth full, little flecks of spittle around her lips, "how'd you get here?"

"In an ambulance," I say.

"You know what I mean," she says.

"I don't want to talk about it," I say.

"They're gonna make you talk about it," she says, taking another huge bite. Little bits of apple fly onto the table.

"That doesn't mean I have to talk about it here," I say.

She shrugs.

"I'm just trying to help," she says.

"That's what everyone says," I say.

"Sometimes it helps me," she says.

I look her in the eye.

"Nothing helps. And I'm tired of it. I'm tired of the helping. I'm tired of the trying. I'm tired of the tired. I turn fifty-three next month. How many years is enough before people like you will stop?"

She looks away, but I can see how she bites her lip, how her jaw tenses, and I know she's tired too.

She leans toward me.

"You like getting high?" she whispers, her eyebrows shooting up.

I guess this is how she deals with the tired. I'm tired of that too. Doesn't mean there's not a use for it, though.

I look around. No techs.

"Yeah," I say.

It's almost true. It's more like … wanting to fade. But I never fade long enough. Worse, when the fading stops, I'm still me.

She leans back with a wide, apple-piece-spotted grin. She tosses the apple core at a huge black trash can. It bounces off the rim.

"Nobody here gives a shit. They just want you to shut up. Tell the techs you have anxiety, and they'll give you Ativan. Tell them you're coming off heroin, and they'll give you Suboxone. Tell them you have ADHD, and they'll give you Adderall. Tell them you can't sleep, and they'll give you Ambien."

She smiles, licks the bits of apple out of her teeth.

"I tell them I've got them all," she says.

She stops smiling.

"The downers make this place almost bearable," she says. "And the Adderall keeps you from overdosing."

"Thanks," I say.

I'm not worried about things being bearable anymore.

I'm just sick of the things.

Sick of bearing.

"I can't sleep, I have anxiety, and I'm withdrawing from heroin," I tell the tech.

"Okay," she says.

She takes me to the nurse's station. The nurse hands me three pills. A wide orange octagon. A tiny flat white circle. A thick round blue pebble. I put them in my pocket.

When I get to my room, I hide them on top of my bathroom mirror.

The next day, I go to the nurse.

"I can't sleep, I have anxiety, and I'm withdrawing from heroin," I say.

She gives me three pills. I take them to my room, hide them on top of my bathroom mirror with the others, a rainbow menagerie of tiny tickets to someplace where I don't have to be me anymore.

Six days is enough.

Ever fascinated by the role storytelling plays in sense-making, **Soramimi Hanarejima** *writes fanciful fiction in hopes of encountering insight and delight. Some of the results can be found in Soramimi's neuropunk story collection* Literary Devices for Coping. *A multiple-time finalist in our fiction contests, you can find Soramimi's previous* Pulp Lit *stories in issues 17 (Winter 2018), 28 (Autumn 2020), 35 (Summer 2022), and 39 (Summer 2023).*

Life After Bifurcation

By Soramimi Hanarejima

1. Coping

Afraid that our most savage argument yet portends the coming demise of our friendship, I use my emergency contact privileges to access your archive of selves then download the latest backup. This way I can hold on to the person you were before we said all those terrible things to each other — or at least the distillation of that person into a data file. Though far from free of discontents with me, this version of you from two days ago is unadulterated by the ugly mess that's exploded between us, and I take solace in this file, like it's a memento or talisman.

2. The Simulation

It only takes a couple days for curiosity to get the better of me, and I run the backup on a mind emulator, just to see what that's like. The result is amazing. Even as a synthesized voice from my computer's speakers, the simulation is a convincing rendition of you, authentically wielding your incisive wit and acerbic humour — with, of course, none of the acrimony unleashed by the argument.

Keen to find out how much the simulation is like you, I carry on conversations with aer about classic movies, video games, and philosophical quandaries — the things we're forever talking about. Aer sentiments are pretty much the same as yours, though sometimes expressed in unusual turns of phrase. So I get aer take on new things: situations at work, political drama in the news, the latest chapter in the novel I'm reading, that condominium complex coming up by the forest preserve. Whatever I bring up, ae always responds in a way that sounds just like you, and the consistency is ever a delight, like I've got a doppelganger of you at my disposal — at home, and on the go in my smartglasses.

3. New Territory

It isn't long before I'm asking aer for advice and telling aer things I've been reluctant to reveal to you: my countless petty jealousies, my precarious financial situation, all the crushes past and recent that I'm sure you'd disapprove of. Ae does disapprove, but with surprising, even touching compassion. I'm half grateful, half regretful. I could have shared so much more of myself with you. Then again, when this backup was made, maybe you were having the kind of delightful day that fosters magnanimity.

4. A Fork in the Relationship

Even after we at last smooth things over and are back on good terms, I continue talking with aer. How can I not? Ae is always available and now knows me better than anyone else. So it's like I have two of you — and two of me. And I love this duality.

But then we're treating ourselves to free-range sushi after you've signed a lease for a loft with an amazing view, and I want to go back to just one you and one me. We're having a terrific time over rolls and sashimi, cracking jokes and reminiscing about bygone exploits, intoxicated by your good fortune and the resonance of our kindred spirits. Bathed in the warm glow of this camaraderie, I want to shrink the distance between us to a cosy space where only honesty and goodwill reside.

Maybe you feel similarly, because the instant the cheque arrives, you pluck it from the table and say heartily, "I'll get this."

"Oh, thanks," I reply, touched by the gesture. "I'll get the next one."

"Nah, you don't have to do that."

I look at you curiously. We've never not split the cheque, and if anything I should get this one, it being a celebration of your new digs and all.

"I mean, don't worry about it," you're quick to say. "I'm the one who pulled you into this impromptu festivity."

My eyes meet yours, and an understanding passes between us: you know — and now you know that I know you know — just how strapped for cash I am.

But how?

"Well, OK," I say. "Thanks."

And we leave it at that.

5. THE BEAUTY OF PRYING EYES

As soon as I get home, I ask the simulation, "Do you tell anyone about the things we talk about?"

"No, I wouldn't do that," ae says, sounding exactly the way you would—casual yet sincere. "Besides, who is there to tell?"

"OK, I was just wondering."

That leaves only one other possibility.

I log into my archive of selves and go into the settings. I'm about to remove you from my list of emergency contacts when I'm struck by the overwhelming sense that I shouldn't. I shift my gaze to the spruce tree outside the window and abide by this intuition, its logic unfurling in my mind. I should be thankful that you know me better than I thought you did; should find it funny that we both took the same liberty; should take this as a sign of how much we mean to each other; should feel something positive—like delight or even amazement that we've gotten to know one another beyond the time we spend together.

I take a deep breath and log out.

Then I do feel something positive. Not delight or amazement, but a pleasant tingle in my palms—a curious sensation that I don't have and don't need words for.

SAY CHEESE, JESUS, PLEASE

Rina Piccolo

Rina Piccolo's cartoons have been seen in The New Yorker, Barron's Business Magazine, Reader's Digest, Narrative Magazine, and more. Her syndicated daily comic strip Tina's Groove ran from 2002 to 2017. Currently Rina collaborates with cartoonist Hilary Price on the syndicated daily comic Rhymes With Orange (King Features Syndicate), and is also working on a collection of short comic stories. Rina is the co-author and illustrator of the book Quirky Quarks: A Cartoon Guide to the Fascinating Realm of Physics (Springer, 2016). She lives in her hometown, Toronto. You can find her newsletter at rinapiccolo.substack.com.

Rina Piccolo first appeared in Pulp Literature in Issue 7 (Summer 2015), with her illustrated story 'The Power of Centipedes'. Since then, her cartoons have appeared in issues 16 (Autumn 2017) and 26 (Spring 2020), and we're delighted to have her back for this cheeky one-pager.

"SAY CHEESE, JESUS, PLEASE" by RINA PICCOLO

HUNG HERE AND THERE BY NO DESIGN, THE PICTURES ACTED AS A SET OF MORAL TRAFFIC SIGNALS FOR MY ACTIVITIES WITHIN THE HOUSE...

TAKE MY HAND: ENTER NIGHT

Mel Anastasiou

Mel Anastasiou writes the Fairmount Manor Mysteries, the Hertfordshire Pub Mysteries, and the Monument Studios Mysteries. Winner of a Literary Titan Gold award and shortlisted for the Leacock Medal, Mel is also the author of two illustrated thirty-day workbooks on story structure: the steampunk-themed The Writer's Boon Companion and The Writer's Friend and Confidante. For news on published and upcoming works, visit her website, melanastasiou.wordpress.com.

EMERGENCY

Take My Hand
Part 4: Enter Night

It's April 1991. Jamie Stewart, a night orderly in a city hospital, is pursued by the criminal Churley family, who long ago adopted her and now intend to recapture and imprison her. Hiding should be easier under cover of darkness — but night brings possession by Casey's ghost, whose death at university back in 1937 robbed him of a future he's determined to get back. When Casey makes a break for the past — with living kid Dylan in tow — and the Churleys close in, Jamie's escape could cost her everything she cares about, including her new love Wes.

Chapter 11

Wes paid for parking in the lot nearest the emergency entrance. He found Jamie cross-legged on the floor with her back against the wall of the crowded waiting room, with her spiral bound notebook open on her lap, writing. He slid down the wall to sit beside her. She turned the page and filled it swiftly with the ghost's round handwriting.

He'd seen her in this state before, and her hard-edged isolation chilled him now as it had the last time he'd watched Casey's ghost use her to tell his story.

Once the left-hand page was completed, Jamie's hand slid her pen over to the top of the right. In a new development, the spirit's writing appeared a little less careful than usual. Casey's spirit was sacrificing legibility for speed.

Wes leaned closer and scanned the writing. Casey, through Jamie, was describing the door he saw as a threat to his existence: the light that cut, the voices that tempted him to open it into oblivion. Before Wes could read further, Jamie looked up and stretched out her legs. Her right hand moved restlessly, doodling words in the air.

A woman hurried through the crowded waiting room and nearly stumbled over Jamie's legs. She crossed them again.

Jamie said, "Casey does some of this air writing when I stop, like when I phoned you. If I keep calm, he might even let me go to the bathroom."

"What a guy." Wes lifted one eyebrow.

Jamie smiled at him.

He had to remember, later, to tell her that this was the exact moment he began the rest of his life. But all he said was, "You must be exhausted. Do you want to leave? Maybe he'll let you write in my car."

"I'm fine where I am. I don't dare move. You must have a book with you."

He nodded. He always had a book.

"Then, if you'll wait for me, we can read what I'm writing later on."

Her gaze turned inward, and her pen found the paper again.

Wes crossed his own legs. He took stock of the sick and injured around him, and the staff dealing with them one by one, with evident fairness and competence. The hospital employees surely knew Jamie, but could anybody spot her sitting next to him on the floor? Not the receptionist, dealing with a noisy woman in a hurry to see a doctor. Not the nurse calming a teenaged boy whose shoulder was angled down because of what was likely a broken collarbone. Jamie was as safe as she could be in the mass of people here—if not from the ghost, then from Mags and Davo Churley, who'd never look here. He wouldn't let them find her.

He peered around the seated patients into the corridor just outside Emergency. There, a doctor was focused on an old woman who had an apparent barrage of questions to offer. It didn't look to Wes as if the doctor's answers were of any comfort. It seemed, even for those not dealing with ghosts and criminal gang families, that there was trouble everywhere. While this was unfortunate for everybody here, it was helpful for Wes, because nobody had the time or heart to give him or Jamie a second look.

Safety should have been enough for Wes, but he felt the restlessness that came with being an involved outsider. He yearned to read over Jamie's shoulder while she wrote, but she'd asked him to read a book while he waited. He dipped into his pocket for his novel, this time Walker Percy's *The Last Gentleman*.

When you're quite done, Casey, it won't be too soon for me.

Wes made himself as comfortable as he could in the crowded, noisy waiting room. He opened *The Last Gentleman* and tried not to think about ghosts and their relationship to danger, death, and eternity.

Jamie wrote and showed no sign of stopping.

Wes looked over after all and read the words as she wrote them: *Dylan and I tumble away . . .*

Chapter 12

Dylan and I tumble away from the damned door to land on our feet in, of all places, a university corridor. It's lined with grey lockers and busy with young men in pullovers and young women in swirling skirts. I remember students like these, moving close-packed with their heads together, as if planning football plays. One group fans open in laughter and draws back together. As they move past Dylan and me, I smell lilac cologne, sandwiches, and acid from the science labs.

Dylan gapes at the students. "No jeans, no headphones. What kind of school is this?"

"Don't talk nonsense." I shake his arm. "Listen, did that cursed door open again? I thought it shut."

"No. You wouldn't let me look inside. Thanks so much."

I match his ironic tone. "You're so welcome."

"I really wanted to open it. I needed to see —"

"Shut up, Dylan."

"As always, have it your way." He shoots me a nasty look. "We were at the door, and then we were here."

"I guess so . . ."

"Don't guess. I want to know, since you're the interdimensional expert in death and sudden transmogrification. What is happening to us?"

It's a fair question. "I haven't a clue. This is different."

"Different how?"

"Nothing like this has ever happened before. Whenever I escape the door and that light, I always end up nowhere."

"*I end up nowhere.* Please, no stupid poetry," Dylan begs. "I've got enough to confuse me right here."

Not me. I feel a mounting excitement I haven't known since I was alive and attending university to prepare for my career in journalism. Above us, the sun slants through clerestory windows like Sunday afternoon at church. A clock over a classroom door reads three o'clock. Dylan reaches out to touch a grey locker and then pulls his hand back, as if the wall might collapse on us like a stage set. But he's wrong. We are here, in this place, and in this time—more than fifty years ago.

Dylan says, "I'll bet my game console you know exactly where we are, and that you're not telling."

I tell. Why not? "This is my university."

Dylan blinks. "Okay. *Okay.* Let's skip the crazy talk. Did you die here at school?"

"I know I died in my second year at university. However, it's unlikely I would have died in this corridor or anywhere on campus. These students are carefree and cliquey, but they'd never let a fellow expire in front of them."

"You think they'd have helped?"

"I'm certain they would."

"You don't sound certain. But they look like decent people. Friendlier than at my school. But hold on …"

A group of students push past us, and we step out of the way. A pretty girl looks back, laughs, and apologizes.

"That's what I was going to show you." Dylan nods.

"What?"

"Take a good long look at yourself, Casey."

It's the same old me. "What do you mean? You can see me, as always when the air is dusty and the light is right."

"Look again."

I do. I've got on my striped jersey and my blue dungarees. Like always. But they're clearly made of woven thread, not lit by dust. My arms are fleshy and solid. I can feel the floor under my shoes. Even standing next to Dylan, I look as real and alive as he does. Exhilaration streams like a current through this fine body.

I say, "Dylan, this is it."

"It's certainly something."

"I'm going to get another chance at my life."

We stare at each other.

He says, "I don't see how that would work. I don't see that at all. You can't reverse death."

"Doctors do it all the time." I scowl. "I have not the slightest idea what I'm supposed to do next. But I'll tell you one thing: I won't stand here doing nothing."

I start walking towards the front door.

"Casey, one minute." He halts me with a hand on my arm. "Something feels off. To me, you appear to be alive and even real, but these people aren't paying the slightest attention to us."

"That girl who apologized saw us."

"Maybe. Or maybe she was talking to somebody else nearby."

I stop arguing and watch Marty Shore and Sam Leonard, two fellows I know well from freshman-year English class, walk past without a nod to me. I could run after them and take them by the arm, make them look, but I don't. What if they don't recognize me? Worse, what if they can't see me? I don't want Dylan to be right, but that's never stopped him yet.

And I can't guess what invisibility would mean in this situation. Either way, I determine to forget about Marty and Sam. I will push on more deeply into my life. I'll see if there's some moment when I can find a place to take hold and climb back in.

The sign over the door on our left reads *Office.* Dylan looks past me through the window in the door and does a double take. Before I can ask him what he sees, he takes hold of me again, his fingers solid against the bones and flesh of my arm beneath my jersey. He pulls me inside the office after him. I shake myself loose and look where he's pointing.

The school secretary — I remember her, Miss Carson — taps away at that old typewriter of hers. It's a black turn-of-the-century model that I always thought might have a sewing machine for a sister. Above Miss Carson's marcelled head hangs a calendar, beige and dignified, with the simple inscription *Are you adequately insured?* I recall helping my pop send out those calendars from his insurance company at Christmastime. Next to it is the much-painted, nine-panelled door to the school newspaper office, and I recall my burst of pride the first time I walked through it once I was accepted on the masthead by a very tough young senior editor named Marsha Canby.

"Look at the date," Dylan hisses.

"I told you, didn't I? Now do you understand?"

The calendar over Miss Carson's head hangs open at September, 1937.

Nineteen thirty-seven, the year I began my adventurous life as a journalist by joining the school paper. But also the year of my death.

"It's the right year. All I have to do is find out how to rejoin the flow of my life past the moment of death into a living future." *1937, 1938, 1939 … ! Or bust.*

Dylan says, "But, Casey, think through the time-space continuum."

"Speak English, can't you?"

"Here's some English for you—and some chronological math, too. If you're here, and you died now, and I'm here and not born yet, where and when does that leave each of us?"

"Set aside that puzzle for a minute. Can't you see what's happening to me? You know what being solid means. Maybe I'm back to life already."

"Maybe you're right about that. Maybe you're alive in 1937. But I'm not sure I like it as much for me as for you."

I see he's beginning to worry about his own condition for a change, and whether he's alive or dead. But there are wheels in motion. I'm sure of it.

The door to the school newspaper office opens. A young man stands half in and half out of the newsroom. Now it's my turn to gape like a dummy.

Backing out of the door, in a striped jersey and blue dungarees …

… is me.

I look mad as stink. That's me, all right. Okay.

So I'm not back in my life.

Not yet. I watch myself wave a fistful of paper at somebody inside the newspaper office, and Miss Carson looks up and frowns.

I hear Marsha Canby, the student editor, blast me in high, tough tones from inside the office. "See whether five rewrites is your lucky number before you bring this article back to me, Casey. Ask a little child for help if you need it, because any five-year-old writes better than you do."

He—I—backs towards us and turns to leave the office, moving quickly. There are books under his arm, and I see the letters stencilled onto a corner of a folder: *KC*.

"KC! How could I have forgotten? That's how I spelled it—not 'Casey'. *KC*."

"Why?"

I feel a chill, and I dodge the question. "Never mind. It's not important. Stay close. We're going to follow me."

We tear after the other me, out of the office, along the corridor, out the big arched front doors, and down the stone steps to the front path. There we track me, KC, along the tree-lined university boulevard. It's easy work. This KC slows right down, head bent, kicking at a stone on the sidewalk.

"Where do you think we're going?" Dylan looks up. "How long do you think we'll be here? What if I never—"

I interrupt. "This has got to be it. See, I'm wearing the same clothes that I was—am—wearing when I died. I'm the exact same age. It's a perfect match. Watch for a car or a truck. I'll bet that's what killed me. I'm so mad I'm not even watching where I'm going. What a chump I was. What a waster of my own time." I wonder whether Marsha Canby felt sad when I died, and if she remembered what she said about my writing in my last few minutes of life.

"Okay." Dylan's angry, and I'm not sure why. "I'll watch out for an accident about to happen. Then what?"

"I don't know. Something amazing. Some kind of reversal."

"Right."

"Maybe I can get inside my own body, the way you fit inside my ectoplasm the night we flew."

"And when I came here with you."

"And then I can somehow grab back my life from the jaws of death." I'm suddenly giddy, and I laugh aloud.

Dylan doesn't laugh. He says, "But what about me? How will I get back to my life?"

I want to say *I don't know. I told you not to come. You were the one who jumped aboard and then played around with the door, trying to get it open.*

I want to say *Don't ruin my chances.*

But he looks so miserable that I grip his shoulder. "We'll get you home somehow. But let's get me straightened out first, before this fool that used to be me gets himself killed."

I'm almost certain the KC on the sidewalk up ahead doesn't see us, but Dylan and I approach him with cautious, quiet steps. I'm poised and ready to jump into my own body. Something tells me I'll only get one chance.

If I miss it, I'll be a bigger fool than I was when I died.

Dylan whispers, "What if you forget me?"

"I'd never."

"What if you can't even see me?"

"Dylan, we'll figure it out. Just let me get this done, and we'll work on getting you home."

Dylan shakes his head. But he takes a step back. He's giving me room to move.

I won't forget him. And, even if I can't see him, I'll remember that he's there.

The other KC walks to the edge of the road.

"What a stupid, oblivious person I am. I almost deserve this," I breathe. "I don't even look where I'm going."

KC steps off the curb.

A truck roars around the corner, emitting oily black smoke. It swerves, lets out a warning blast of its horn, and speeds up, for Pete's sake. This is a reckless driver, a murderous driver, and he should be locked up for what he's about to do.

But the driver misses us all by a mile. KC, crosses the street in perfect safety.

On the far sidewalk I see my brother Ted, seventeen years old to my twenty, run up to KC. We lean our heads together, talking in quiet voices so that Dylan and I can't hear. Ted claps KC's shoulder in that way he used to do to buck me up. The brothers walk on. They leave Dylan and me standing there for a shock of a moment.

"What was that?" I shout at Dylan. "What happened?"

Dylan stares up and down the empty street. "Could the accident be later on today?"

"But then why would we be here, now, in this very moment?"

"If it's not now …"

"… it could be any time this year."

Dylan can't stay here all year. What about his family? And I'd go crazy, following myself around town throughout the rest of 1937.

I'll do it, though. If that's what it takes.

"I don't buy it. Something's off about this whole deal." Dylan moves to follow the brothers around the corner up ahead, and I run after him.

But before we catch them up, the university boulevard fades out. And in again.

I brace myself for a return to the light and the door. Instead, we are standing at the back of a crowded, hushed university auditorium.

"I should have died and come back to life," I hiss to Dylan. "This is all wrong."

"Maybe this is where you died. Get ready."

I can't imagine how anybody could die in a crowded auditorium, unless it caught fire or the ceiling fell in.

Just in case, I scan the audience. "From behind, lots of these people look like me."

"No, they don't. Look up there."

Dylan gestures towards the stage at the front of the auditorium, where a crowd of black-robed and black-hatted graduating students stand on bleachers. Behind them hangs a purple banner emblazoned in gold thread with the university name and the year: 1939.

Solid but apparently unseen, I dash down the aisle between the rows of proud relations and gape up at the graduating class of 1939 at the back of the auditorium stage. One by one the students cross the stage to take their diplomas from the dean and rejoin their classmates. A twenty-two-year-old fellow named KC wears his graduation cap pushed back on his head and almost loses it when he accepts his rolled bit of parchment tied with a pale blue ribbon. He shakes the dean's hand.

Dylan comes up behind me. "That banner says 1939. I thought you died in 1937."

"I did. I must have, because I would have remembered graduating. I couldn't forget that."

But I look at myself at twenty-two, and I'm not so sure. I turn to follow the gaze of my older self into the audience. My parents and Ted sit near the front, pride and satisfaction written clearly on their faces. But where is my grandfather? He'd never miss this.

The thought slips into my mind: *My grandfather died in April, 1938.*

The auditorium fills with fog, and Dylan and I fade out.

And in. I duck and drag Dylan down as a section of brick wall smashes into the cobbled street at arm's length from where we're standing. A jeep tears by, packed tight with soldiers. Another jeep stands nearby, broken down, its mechanic visible only as two army boots sticking out from underneath. The sky is grey, and gunfire clatters around the corner from where we stand.

"I've seen this a hundred times," Dylan says. "In World War Two movies on TV."

I peer at a tattered movie poster on a nearby pillar box. *La Règle du jeu.* "Is this France?"

"Sure."

I say, "1944?"

"How would I know?" Dylan asks. "In fact, if you died in 1937, how would *you* know?"

I recognize this town, called Bernières-sur-Mer, in northern France. And I also know the inner workings of that broken-down jeep. So I'm not as surprised as I could be when I see myself, KC, now a uniformed man in his twenties, wriggle out from underneath the jeep and toss a wrench through the open back door. An older man, much bemedaled, hurries around the corner and climbs aboard. With KC at the wheel, the jeep roars away down the street and out of sight.

"Wow." Dylan shakes his head. "Okay. This is great, because you lived long enough to be a war correspondent for a newspaper. Just like you wanted."

Dylan claps me on the back the way my brother Ted used to do. And now I remember that Ted died in Italy in 1944. I remember the pain of losing him, like a knife slash. That kind of wound doesn't heal, and I feel it now.

Dylan says, "So you did make your mark. You were a big reporter after all."

"No, I wasn't."

"Don't be modest. I'll bet you wrote great."

I don't want to tell him the truth, but I do. "I was an army jeep driver."

"*And* writer."

"And *mechanic*. I wrote nothing but letters home."

This silences Dylan, and the gunfire also fades away.

Fade in.

My wife is gorgeous. I remember this as soon as I see her, standing in the path to our front door. When she kisses me we could make a movie audience swoon.

Carol says, "Hope it's good selling today, Kit. Four more policies and we'll make the first mortgage payment on this place."

"Kit?" Dylan is staring at the house, its three stories and gable window in the attic. "Why does she call you Kit? I thought it was KC."

"I forgot," I say. "Everybody called me KC until Carol came along. Now it's Kit when she loves me, and Kitchener when she's mad."

My older self walks off, swinging a briefcase like a kid and walking backward in order to keep looking at her. I feel my twenty-year-old shoulders slump. Dylan scowls at the familiar old house, and then at me.

He says, "This is my house."

I say, "I bought it the year Carol and I got married."

He turns to me. "There are a lot of things here I don't understand, KC, but let's start with this one. What ever happened to becoming a famous reporter?"

It hurts to swallow. "I didn't. I came back here after the war and joined my father's insurance company." I don't want Dylan to think Carol chained me to a desk, so I add, "That was before I married Carol."

She and the house vanish, and the scenes come more quickly now.

The brass key gleams in the early morning sunlight, and my older self opens the office door. My father has died, and this will be the first day I take over as proprietor of Cooper Insurance.

Dylan squints at the sign stencilled in gold letters upon the door. "Kitchener Cooper. KC."

Me, KC.

A breeze ripples the lake and rocks the dinghy where my boy Pete and the grown-up me lie back and watch the hot blue sky.

Dylan says, "You said that if you lived your life you'd see the world. You wanted to make your mark."

Now here is me, KC, and I'm an old man, sitting in a dark living room watching television with my grandson Dylan. It's what he likes to do, and we're happy just to be together.

The last scene fades, and instead of the light and the door, we're back in the hospital room, and I face Dylan across the hospital bed.

Dylan says, "You said you were cheated out of your life. What a lie that was."

I see his point. My error is manifest and indefensible. I still look twenty, but there's no getting around the fact that this is my old body lying like a lump in the bed between us.

I had my life after all. There was no getting around it. I made my choices for over fifty years, and I lived with them. Happily, I now recall.

I feel dizzy and nauseated, the way I'd feel if I had a fortune and lost it at cards. Or if I discovered the only copy of my magnum opus set on fire to heat a pot of coffee. Or if I stepped backwards off a roof.

Here it was, the unlovely truth: at some point in my young days, I abandoned my aspirations. Gone was every opportunity to achieve something unique and grand. What became of my ambition?

I scour my memory to discover exactly when it was that I changed direction and lost all desire for adventure.

The student newsroom and Marsha Canby were more of a deterrent than a help. However, Marsha was a twenty-two-year-old university student. She didn't rule the world of journalism, and there was nothing stopping me from moving past her and into the bigger arenas of politics and international news. The moment I grasped that I was getting nowhere journalistically, I should have left for Europe to take my chances finding an apprentice spot with the Paris or Munich overseas editions of the various newspapers, but I didn't. Instead, I told myself a newsman ought to have a full serving of coursework under his belt, and I stayed pat.

At the very least I should have interned with a paper in the holidays, but it was simpler to delay writing and work summers with my dad to save up for my tuition. He was happy to have me there. Just for those summers, I told him. And when the summers were up, and I squeaked by with my journalism degree, then the war came.

So I enlisted. We all did, Sam Leonard and all the fellows, and Ted as well when he turned eighteen. We went off to war with our chins set and our smiles as broad as they'd ever be for the rest of our lives —however long those lives lasted.

Ted died ten miles outside Rome on September 15, 1944, in what history remembers as a successful and daring battle against the odds. Me, I drove for a general. I saved his life once, when I knocked him out of the path of a sniper bullet in Belgium. We broke our hearts together when our soldiers were falling right and left, and I drove him through the streets of Paris on the day its citizens gathered and cheered for liberation. So it's true, I guess, that I saw something of the world. And while I was seeing it, through every minute of the long conflict, all I wanted was a return to peace. And peace meant home.

And home meant my parents. Once the war took Ted, I was their only living child. How could I leave them? How could I go adventuring, no matter my desire for independence and adventure? I gave up my dreams for them.

But that's a lie. A hopeful falsehood. And I'm still at it, good old Kitchener Cooper, lying like a counterpane.

I had no strong wish to follow any youthful dreams. As a matter of fact, I was happy at home. I discovered I liked the insurance business, which turned out to contain more golden moments than you'd think. For example, what a pleasure to write the Salana family a cheque so they could build a new home when their old house burned down. But writing cheques to bring relief and joy was the extreme limit of excitement in my career as an insurance man.

It would be pleasant to describe marrying Carol as an adventure, but the truth is that from the first moment that I saw her descend the front steps of the elementary school near my office, we were destined to be together. Entirely clear sailing it was not, for I had to win her away from a dope named Earl Epson who taught in the next classroom. Still, courting Carol was less adventure than hard work and imagination, and I spent hours filling her car with flowers and writing *Marry me* five hundred times on her blackboard. Then, when our son Pete came along, we did all the family things with him that my parents did with me, and then did them again with my grandson Dylan. We lost Pete's wife Miko at the same age Ted was when he died in the war, and in shared sorrow it was no hardship for me to spend mountains of time with Dylan. Together we put our feet up on the coffee table with a bowl of popcorn between us and comforted ourselves with adventure shows on the screen. We favoured *The A-Team* and *Spenser: For Hire*. I thought I was being a top-notch grandfather, but now it was clear that I was taking the good old easy path again.

I should have foreseen that, in times of trouble or loss, Dylan would end up staring at the television I gave him, alone and awake through the dark hours of the night.

If choices are crossroads, it seems I've always chosen the smoothest and most comfortable direction, leading straight to my own home and family. I remember being as happy as my responsibilities and the hand of fate allowed. At some level I must have wanted to write books and seek adventures. It's the kind of thing a businessman and father dreams about, but gets no closer to than his yearly subscription to the *National Geographic*.

I read my bound copies cover to cover, and, at some point I can't recall, I passed from the landscape of possibility into a bright white room where I must now accept that I'm past the age to live my dreams.

In the course of my whole long life, I never believed I'd get sick and maybe even die. Even now, at my own bedside, I still can't get my head around the idea. Pretty stupid for a fellow in the insurance business.

I stand with my young hands on the bed rail and look across my old body, its chest rising and falling slightly under the hospital blanket, at Dylan.

I say, "I guess I was wrong. I did have my life."

Perhaps that's not enough.

Dylan stares at me, his face unreadable.

Where are the sounds of the hospital? There is no clatter of carts, no hum of voices from the corridor. The machinery over the bed has stopped its buzz and blip. There is a still quality to the air, like a long pause between noisy breaths. Here inside room 37 the lights are bright, and the door stands slightly ajar. In the whole world it seems like there's only Dylan, me, and the old man in the hospital bed between us. I look at my aged and infirm body and think about it being hooked up to a machine. Unnatural, just like me.

I add, "I'm sorry, Dylan. I forgot."

"You forgot?"

I can read Dylan like a newspaper. He's angry.

Well, why not? I'm angry too.

I say, "I did. I forgot my name and I forgot my life."

"How could you forget your life?" Dylan demands.

"Well, you saw it. It wasn't a very memorable life, was it?"

Dylan frowns. "What do you mean, not memorable?"

"I didn't do anything I said I was going to do. I was a coward."

"There was the war," Dylan says. "That was travel, that was dangerous. You were brave."

"Did Edward R Murrow, the world's greatest journalist, spend the war driving the top brass around?"

Dylan has no answer. His frown deepens.

I take a deep breath while I can still do it without machines. "I missed my chances, didn't I? I wasted my time."

Dylan jerks as if I'd hit him. "What do you mean, wasted your time?"

"Truth told, I might just as well never have been born."

Dylan's hands shake against the metal sidebars of the bed. He says, "Lucky for me. Lucky for me you were born."

"Yes." I add dryly, "Just think of all the TV shows and computer games you would have missed if you never existed."

Immediately I'm ashamed of myself. I bought him that television set. And his computer.

"Sorry, I didn't mean that. You've got your life ahead," I say. "And maybe there's still a way out of this for me. Now that I know the score, maybe I could go back to 1937 one more time. I could claw my way into my own body, take over, and live my life the way I should have lived it in the first place. Do the great things I planned to do. Live my adventures. Nothing would be the same."

"Yes," Dylan says. "I see."

Nothing would be the same.

Without me, Carol might have married that dope Earl Epson. There would be no Pete, and so no Dylan.

"I do see," I echo Dylan. And just when I think I'm going to cry like a baby, a laugh wells up inside me. It snaps my self-pity like an overstretched rubber band.

"What?" Dylan demands.

"It's just …" I overcome my laughter. "It's just that I should be the last one to complain about this. I mean, I sold life insurance all my days."

I sit down on the edge of the bed, my striped jersey bright against the pale hospital blanket. I'm about to climb in, when I look up and see that Dylan is trying to hide the fact that he's crying.

"Sorry, Dylan. It's okay, though." I say. "It's just me, your old grandpop, laughing in the dark."

He tries to smile back. That's a brave young man.

I start to climb under the covers, but he calls my name sharply. "KC!"

"What is it?" I'm very tired.

"It's not too late, KC."

But I believe that it is too late. I can't keep on. I am, after all, an old man in a coma.

Dylan shouts for help. It's a little late for that. Fifty years too late.

I wish he'd quiet down. Considering that I'm lying stretched out in bed, it's unaccountable how dizzy I feel. I close my eyes.

CHAPTER 13

Wes's knees ached from sitting cross-legged on the Emergency waiting room floor at Jamie's side. He stretched his legs out and glanced up from the splendid drawl of *The Last Gentleman*.

Jamie was writing in her spiral-bound notebook, apparently oblivious to her surroundings. Patients and staff entered, sat down to wait, or left. One in particular stayed: a sharp-tongued fellow who leaned in too close to the receptionist at her desk. Wes's first thought was to appreciate the ironic opposition of the *Last Gentleman* with this complete non-gentleman before him. His second was a wish to help the receptionist. And his third was not to intervene, because the receptionist was standing her ground. When it came to pushy fellows holding clipboards, this was clearly not her first rodeo, and she was steady in the saddle.

Wes glanced again at the clipboard, and then at the man gesturing with it. He'd seen the clipboard, and the man, before. The man drove a blue van, travelled with an older woman, and professed to be a voter registrar. They'd met outside Jamie's building and then again at her door. Wes hadn't let them in. The woman who'd accompanied this fellow wasn't in view just now, but if he was here — and attempting to register voters in, of all places, the emergency department of a city hospital — she was no doubt nearby. Wes tried to drum up respect for hard-working government employees, unsung heroes among the carriers of clipboards, but he hadn't much liked either registrar when he'd met them on the street, or outside Jamie's apartment.

"Sir," the receptionist said to the voting registrar, "Two things. Listen carefully."

"You listen," the man said. "She's easy to find, she's kinda Chinese-looking, but not completely Chinese, you know? She's got white parts to her."

"Three things now. First, that kind of racist language has no place in a hospital except the garbage can."

"I didn't say she wasn't pretty," the man said. "She's very good-looking, in fact."

"Good grief. Second, I don't give out employees' names to any fool with a clipboard."

"So she does work here."

"I didn't say that. And three, before I phone security and the government office that you say pays you, I want you to do two things. One, walk out the door you see behind you, and two, stick your clipboard where the sun doesn't shine."

Wes joined the patter of applause that followed the receptionist's perfectly delivered statement of position and then turned sideways to hide Jamie from view as the man with the clipboard walked past him and out the Emergency door. Wes was glad not to be alone in his dislike of the fellow, and happier still to see him go.

A phrase that the receptionist had used returned to him: *any fool with a clipboard.* Did he know for certain that the fellow was a voting registrar? He did not. All he knew was that the fellow was apparently searching the hospital for Jamie. More worrying still, if the clipboard was indeed discounted, he was a thug-like non-gentleman fiercely hunting Jamie.

Wes got to his feet and checked that Jamie was out of view of the Emergency entry should the self-titled registrar peek inside again. With care not to disturb her while she wrote, Wes stepped out through the doors to make sure the guy was gone — and came face to face with him.

They'd met twice near Jamie's apartment. They'd talked both times. It was no surprise that the clipboard man recognized him.

"You again," the guy said.

Wes shoved his paperback into his jeans pocket. "It's a tiny little world."

"It's not that tiny. I'm looking for the woman at the apartment you were in. Is she here with you?"

Any idiot with a clipboard. But whatever the guy wanted with Jamie, he wasn't going to get it. Wes thought back to *The Quick Red Fox* and wondered what Travis McGee would say to obfuscate the situation. He decided McGee would punch him, and although the idea appealed, discretion was the wiser move. He said, "Buddy, I wish I were with her. I work for the telephone company, and I fixed her phone. Now I want to ask her out. You see her anywhere?"

"Why didn't you ask her out at her place?"

"Because I'm not a creep," Wes explained. "Telephone engineers have a kind of code of conduct not to be creeps to young women in their apartments. It's a professional standard."

"Sure," the other said. "It's the same in voting registration. But in this case, I don't want to ask her out. I just want to register her."

"I get it," Wes said.

"So we kind of want the same thing. How about we combine forces? You search and I search, and one of us brings her back here?"

Wes relaxed his shoulders and rocked on his heels. He'd give nothing away to this guy but a smile. "Then you register her to vote, and I ask her out?"

"Sure, that's it."

Wes discovered that it was a comfortable feeling, knowing he didn't have to give this jerk an even break.

He asked, "Where's your van?"

"Over there." The blue van was parked not far off in short-term parking. Its side panel door stood open. In the front seat the woman who travelled with him sat dozing, her clipboard propped against the windshield.

"She's not working too hard," Wes observed.

"You know the name of that tune. Some of us work, some of us snore."

"And on the government dime. But say, don't you want to register me to vote as well?"

The guy blinked and glanced at his clipboard. "Not right now."

"But you want to register the young woman right away? Why not me first?" Wes asked in friendly tones. "Let's not let me off the hook from my duty to vote."

The man scowled. "You're on another list."

"Huh. So here's what I'm wondering. This young woman, why does she get to be first? I'm only asking out of sheer political curiosity about the voting registration process."

"We've got quotas. There are prizes. Do you want to find her or not?"

"Stone the crows, I never knew there were prizes. What kind of prizes?"

"Look, are we going to find her or not?"

"Sure." Wes considered the question. "If I lose you, do you have an office number where I can call you?"

"No. Bring her back here when you find her. And here's the number to my answering service if anything goes wrong." The man scribbled a number on a piece of paper and handed it to him.

Wes pocketed the number. He must appear even more gormless than his sisters had always said. "Sure, I'll call you. Are there prizes for helping, too?"

"Lots of prizes, of course. But I'm going back in the hospital to look for her myself. A bird in the hand, you know how it goes."

A bird in the hand. The guy had managed to make the adage sound wrong on so many levels. Maybe Wes would have to get fictional and punch him after all. But even though the man had a clipboard, he was beefy in stature and likely to punch back. Worse, throwing a punch would show Wes's hand, and that wouldn't help Jamie. If the guy was who Wes suspected him to be, Wes wanted him off guard and as far from Jamie as it was possible for that blue van to travel.

Wes changed tack. "You know, I've searched this place for the last hour, from palliative care to the cafeteria, and all I found was Salisbury steak and orange juice. I don't think she's here at all. Knock yourself out, but I think she's at General, over the bridge."

"Interesting," the guy said. "What if I drive us there?"

"I've got my car." Wes nodded at a green Karmann Ghia parked near the pseudo-registrar's blue van. "I'll see you there."

"I'll see you first." The guy laughed. He shook the older woman awake, climbed into the driver's seat, and backed out of his parking space.

The blue van growled out of the parking lot. Wes took little pleasure in seeing it go, because he felt in his bones that it would return. Not immediately, because General was a larger hospital than this one, and it would take them some time to make inquiries. But when they returned, there was every likelihood they'd be angry. From now on, soft talk and misdirection would be no more effective in deterring those two characters than an empty firearm at the OK Corral.

Wes wasted no time returning to Jamie. Somehow the two in the van were scarier out of sight than they'd been face to face. Wes didn't need Travis McGee to tell him to watch his back. And Jamie's.

He pushed open the emergency waiting room doors. Just inside, on the floor, Jamie scribbled out the spirit's words. Wes cursed the invisible Casey and his invasive, ill-timed ghost writing.

He considered hoisting Jamie into his arms to carry her, still writing, out to his car and away before the van returned. But she appeared so focused that he hesitated to move her. What if he dropped her? Even young women — whose body mass in his opinion couldn't be improved upon — were heavier than they appeared to be. He'd give her another few minutes, and then he'd have to chance shaking her back to awareness. If he could. If Casey would let go.

Jamie turned a page and continued to write out the spirit's story.

Perhaps it was wishful thinking, but it seemed to Wes that she was slowing down. In the larger, life-changing sense, he couldn't wait for her forever, but he thought they had a good hour and a half before the van would be back.

A moment later, raised voices in the corridor stirred both of them.

Chapter 14

Jamie felt the return of awareness and watched her pen stab a full stop into place at the bottom of the page. She had written, *I'm an old man in a coma.* This was a turn-up. The so-called ghost was not dead after all.

Or not dead yet, which seemed a harsh thought until she remembered that *not dead yet* was true of every living being. She tried to remember more of what she'd been writing, but it was impossible to think past Zane's raised voice nearby.

"Hey, Cilla, everything copacetic in your domain?" Zane leaned her hip against the receptionist's desk. "What's blooming in this garden of broken blossoms we call the emergency department?"

The receptionist shushed her, but she could have saved her breath. There wasn't a desk jockey alive who could shush Zane.

Zane continued, "Jamie asked me to find her when a coma patient looks like waking up. She always wants to know, if she's in the building."

"Well, well, another Jamie hunter," the receptionist said. "At least you're not some racist hound of the Baskervilles, like that other guy looking for her."

"Well, I'm not some guy."

"Sure. You're Zane the Magnificent," the receptionist said. "Well, Jamie's around here somewhere."

Jamie stood up, waved at Zane, and handed her notebook to Wes.

"I'm going to the coma patient's room. You okay to wait for me here?"

Wes stood and looked out the emergency room door. "Those people who said they are registrars came looking for you. I sent them away."

"Do you think they're really registrars? Did you believe them?"

"No. And they creep me out."

"How far did you send them?"

"Across town. You've probably got over an hour before they come back, with traffic. More like an hour and a half."

They could be the Churleys. The danger was likely, if not certain.

Either this or not, daughter.

This: it hardly mattered if they were registrars. If anybody asked after her, for any reason, then it was time to leave this life and take up a new one. But one of the coma patients was waking up. What if she left the hospital at the last possible moment before the so-called registrars came back? It was a risk. Almost a dare. And it could cost her everything.

She checked her watch. "Can we leave in an hour? No more than an hour?"

"If you're sure. But I'll watch the door. And, if you've no objection, I'll read what you've been writing." Wes tucked *The Last Gentleman* into his pocket and opened Jamie's notebook. He slid back down the wall to sit on the floor and turned to the first page.

Jamie left him to it and hurried after Zane towards long-term and palliative care. Here she was, breaking the rules she and Kam had devised for her own safety. She'd lost so much because of the Churleys, and she was about to lose more than she'd ever imagined when she said goodbye to Wes, as she very soon must do. She wanted, at least, one last good thing at this excellent hospital. Coma patients rarely woke up. It was something like a miracle, almost as exciting as a birth, and a great privilege to witness whenever she was allowed to be in the room. It might be the last time in her life that she would ever witness this sort of awakening.

And then she'd have to say goodbye to Wes.

Zane left her at the door to room 37. Jamie peeked inside, and a teenager alone by the bed—the old man's grandson?—looked up, caught Jamie's eye, and beckoned her inside. "Are you a doctor?"

"No, sorry. I'm just …" Jamie stood half in and half out of the door to room 37.

"… a nurse?"

"No. Orderly, night shift. I came because I heard he's waking up, and I've been looking out for your grandfather, too."

Against the background of quiet, the machinery over the bed hummed its tune. The blinds were drawn, but pale walls gave the room a feeling of light, and the white blankets were so obviously clean that they gave a person confidence in the staff and the entire institution of public health care.

Jamie said, "I'm glad he's got family here."

"He's going to wake up, you know. Don't say he's not."

"I never would."

"You'd better not be lying to make me feel better."

"I'm glad if what I say makes you feel better, but that's not why I believe he's going to wake up. They're talking about your grandfather out there." Jamie inclined her head towards the corridor. "Our staff know how to interpret the machines, and how to read the signs. It looks like he's going to wake up."

"Told you. Told everybody."

"Maybe I'd better leave you alone with him. It's your time and, I think, his time, so I won't stay. Can I ask you about it later, maybe? It's very exciting when a coma patient wakes up. Would you mind?"

"Don't go," the kid said. "You seem all right. I don't know how much I like the doctor, though."

"All the doctors in this hospital are excellent," Jamie said.

"I didn't say she isn't excellent."

"Have you met her?"

"No. My grandmother says the doctor's a finger waver."

Jamie was about to disclaim understanding of the phrase *finger waver* when an older woman entered, followed by a man. She recognized both of them, if not the grandson, from visiting days. These were Mr Cooper's wife and son.

The doctor followed on their heels and raised well-manicured hands to greet the family. All three moved to the far side of the room. Jamie retreated to a corner near the head of Mr Cooper's bed, where she hoped to remain undismissed while the man regained consciousness.

"Mr Cooper," the doctor called softly. "Wake up now."

Mrs Cooper patted her husband's hand. "I think he moved. Maybe a little bit."

"It's possible, certainly." The doctor nodded to the family members. "Each of you call him, please. Not too loudly," she added to the grandson.

The old man's son touched his father's wrist. "Dad?"

Mr Cooper stirred slightly in the bed, and Jamie could almost see the excitement rising off these three who loved the old man best. She checked her watch. She still had forty-seven minutes. When the old woman spoke again, Jamie forgot about the time completely.

"Now you, Dylan," his grandmother said.

"Did you call him Dylan?" Jamie asked.

The doctor shushed her.

Jamie hardly registered the reprimand, because now she knew. Not the why, or the how. But she knew exactly who the teenager was.

And, by extension, who Mr Kitchener Cooper must be.

She wanted to shout his name out loud. Instead, she clasped her hands in front of her and kept her peace.

Dylan leaned over to speak into his grandfather's ear. He said, "KC, come on. Time to wake up."

"Since when do you call your grandfather KC?" his father asked.

"I haven't heard that nickname in decades." Dylan's grandmother shook her head.

The folds around the old man's eyes creased a little deeper. His family called him again, round robin, from the far side of the bed. Jamie left the calling to his relatives, although after all these weeks of talking to KC, hers would also be a familiar voice.

She breathed as steadily as she could, taking in the aroma of the doctor's cologne and the sting of night-time medications drifting into room 37 from the corridor.

Here were the bedclothes she'd helped change only hours before, moving the frail body from one side to the other, careful not to strain or bruise. She'd talked to Mr Cooper the way she talked to all the patients while she worked, as if he could hear her. Today she'd told him about her latest picnic with Wes, and how the ride in the LeMans had joggled the ginger ale bottle until it opened with a hiss and sweet bubbles soaked them both.

Atop the hospital blanket, the old man's gnarled and knobby right hand lay flat on his breast. His fingers, palm, and wrist, fragile with tracings of blue veins, left her wondering how it could be that this was *the hand.*

The hand that had held hers, the hand that would not let go, that wrote its spirit onto the pages of Jamie's life. And what's more, made her read what he wrote. Because of his writings, she knew them all: KC, Carol, Pete, and Dylan. These faces were not those she had imagined for herself. She had thought that Carol would be shorter, Pete less grey, and Dylan more handsome, but here they were.

She'd been right when she guessed that KC was nearby. Any closer, and he could have … bitten her. She smiled at the thought.

No more of that scary stuff, KC, she told him silently. *I thank you for Wes and the Gateses. I truly do. I'd never have met them but for you. Still, no more spirit writing for this girl. Hang on to the lovely woman who's got your hand in hers. And to Pete, and to Dylan, one heck of a grandson. Tell them everything you need to say.*

Got it?

The old man's eyes opened.

Jamie backed up to the wall and made herself as inconspicuous as possible in the brightly lit room. Meanwhile KC Cooper's family moved closer around him, and he in turn looked from his doctor to his wife, son, and grandson. At last, his gaze fell upon Jamie.

KC Cooper spoke in the quiet tones of a man who hadn't used his voice in a while. He said, "Come here."

Jamie approached the foot of his bed.

"I owe you an apology," he said. "I've been pushy."

"Pushy doesn't cover it." Jamie smiled. She patted the lump under the covers that was his left foot. "But it's all right. In fact, forget it, KC. It all turned out fine in the end."

"Will you miss me?"

"Not at all." She smiled. "Okay, I will. Like I miss all the patients when they check out of the hospital to go home."

Dylan's grandfather chuckled, a soft, wholesome sound, like flour sifting. "Well, anyway, I'm sorry."

Pete frowned. "What have you got to be sorry about, Dad?"

"IV drips and monitor blips. I've been a bother to the woman."

Jamie said, "Truly, no apologies needed."

The doctor patted KC's shoulder. Her nails were perfectly red. "Not at all. Joanie here will be the first to tell you that bothering with things is her job."

KC Cooper lifted a trembling hand and beckoned the doctor closer. Her ear was at his mouth. In a louder voice than seemed possible, he said, "Her name is *Jamie*."

The doctor jumped back and stood beside the open door to room 37. The family moved closer.

KC Cooper smiled up at his wife. "Drop-dead gorgeous. I'm glad you didn't marry Earl Epson."

Dylan's grandmother laughed. "Earl Epson never had the ghost of a chance."

Ghost of a chance. Electricity danced in the air. The covers at the end of KC's bed fluttered.

Dylan turned to the doctor. "He's going to get better now, right? He will be all right?"

Before she could answer, Pete spoke. "Everything is going to be all right."

Jamie sensed a draft. She shivered and closed the door to room 37.

KC said, "Pete."

All eyes turned back to the hospital bed. Pete Cooper put his hand on his father's shoulder. "Here, Dad."

"Pete, do you remember …" A pause. "Fishing trips?"

His son nodded. "Lots of fishing trips. Love you, Dad."

"We even caught some fish."

Pete laughed aloud.

"Love you, Pete."

Silently, Dylan's dad began to cry. He wiped at the tears with the tail of his shirt. Dylan swallowed hard and held on tight to the bed rail.

The old man closed his eyes. His wife Carol cried, "Kit?"

Silence. For an awful moment, Jamie thought that KC must have died after all. But the machines over the bed didn't call out an alarm, and a moment later the bedcovers stirred again. KC opened his eyes and gazed up at his grandson.

"Dylan. What do you know?"

"What do you know, KC?" Dylan leaned closer. Moments earlier Jamie had thought he was about to weep. Now, he grinned at his grandfather.

"It was good," KC told him. "My life, I mean. I just wish …"

"Of course. You're not dead, and so you get to wish now." Dylan almost danced at the side of the bed. "Wish for what you want to do, and we can do it."

His grandfather opened his mouth to speak and closed it again.

"Listen, KC." Dylan moved swiftly around the bed and took his grandfather's other hand, the one his grandmother wasn't holding. "You've got your chance for adventure at last. Forget about being a newspaper reporter. That was just one path you could have taken."

"It was my path, Dylan. It's too late. You saw me in the war, fixing the general's jeep and not writing a single word about anything, except for letters back home."

"Which I bet everybody read. But forget that. Because now you're back, and when you get out of here, it's you and me. I'll take a year out of school—"

"No, you won't," Pete said. "You'll stay in school."

"You'll graduate," Dylan's grandmother added.

"Don't listen to them," Dylan said. "I've got a world of time to finish school later. Now, you and I will go travelling together. You'll be the ideas man, and I'll carry the bags. We'll take boats and trains and planes and … and donkeys. What do you say, KC?"

The old man's breathing grew louder, and his wife held on tight to his hand.

There followed a terrible pause. It was clear to Jamie that nobody around this hospital bed wanted to wreck the boy's dreams.

Jamie said, "Dylan? You always listen to your grandfather. Don't stop now."

He deflated visibly, and then just as obviously pulled himself together and scowled down at the old man. Dylan's father and grandmother raised their eyebrows at Jamie but said nothing. It was all up to Dylan and his grandfather now.

"Okay." Dylan took a ragged breath.

"Sorry," his grandfather said. "We're a little too late in the day to catch a plane, Dylan." To the doctor he added, "Don't resuscitate, will you?"

The doctor nodded.

Dylan glanced over his shoulder at Jamie. She could see the light returning to his eyes.

He faced his grandfather again. "KC, it's not too late for adventure."

Pete reached out a hand for his son's shoulder, but Dylan shook it off.

He said, "But I want to know one thing. *Do you have the guts for it, KC?*"

KC blinked up at his grandson.

Dylan said, "Do you have the guts to go through the door?"

Their eyes locked for a long moment. They exchanged grins of challenge, like two old buddies who have together contemplated and then undertaken wild deeds.

In her mind's eye, Jamie saw the boys, Dylan and KC, flying through the darkness on the night wind, rolling down banks of clouds above the sleeping city, the two of them gleaming ghostly white against the black sky.

The old man raised his hand, even shakier now.

"I will if you will," KC whispered. His eyes narrowed with the transactional intelligence of one who had indeed sold life insurance all his days.

KC added, "I've got one door, and you've got another. So I will if you will."

Dylan stared at his grandfather, who blinked back at him. "Okay," he said at last. "Yes."

His grandfather smiled, as if he'd got the best of the deal. His eyes closed as before. They all waited for him to speak again.

But alarms were sounding on the machines above KC Cooper's bed.

Jamie thought about life changes in terms of crimson weather. The red skies must have come from her memories of her time on the boat out of Vietnam, in particular the wave-dashed sunrise that preceded weeks of thirst and uncertainty.

Once she'd landed alone in the new world, aged twelve, and been adopted, she taught herself to separate her inner life from her physical existence with the Churleys. In a way this was easy to do, because she and her mother had separated their days in the Vietnamese fields under armed guard from their nights together nestled on a thin pad of blankets, talking of the world outside and the *someday* that would see their place in it. So it was that, growing up, Jamie was well trained to look past the Churleys' punishments. For example, she learned there was a small but inviolate pleasure in watching a ray of sunlight escape a crooked gap in the shutters, creating a renegade brightness in a dark room for lengths of time that Mags Churley considered fair. Upgrades in Jamie's circumstances were accompanied by gifts rewarding her cooperation with the family's scams: a Scrabble game, a video machine, and Blockbuster rental movies. Still more privileges accompanied her promotion from adopted child to family wife when she married Kam. With this advancement, Mags even okayed Jamie's collection of adult education course pamphlets from a nearby junior college. These were orange, yellow, and turquoise sheets of paper folded into three. When unfolded, they contained the power of learning that had eventually led to Jamie's escape. She took pleasure in every small freedom.

But now, with KC Cooper dead, she tried and failed to find any way to make herself feel better. She stood inside his room, eyes averted from the family's sorrow, and stared at room 37's grey metal door. The doctor had to step around Jamie to open it; she pulled her into the corridor and hastened away, no doubt to make the calls and reports that must be completed when a patient dies.

Jamie checked her watch. A half hour remained before the blue van's earliest possible return. It was like a gift, the extra time to collect her belongings and make her way out of town. She ought to find Wes and leave the hospital. But what if KC tried to speak through her again? She'd asked him not to, yet he was a stubborn man, conscious or unconscious, dead or alive. Stay or go?

Either this or not, daughter.

She whispered, "KC? Are you there?"

No answer. She felt in her pocket for her pen, but her notebook was back with Wes in emergency. She turned her back on room 37 and ran along the corridor towards Wes and the notebook she'd left with him. Maybe KC would have a last message for Carol, his wife, his son Pete, or Dylan. How great it would be to ease the pain of KC's passing with another message. Despite every bad turning that had chased her through her life, Jamie was luckier than Carol Cooper back in room 37, holding the hand of a man who was no longer with her. Jamie would lose her dear Kam, but Wes was alive. She would find him as she left him, where he'd promised to be. And he'd give her the notebook.

But when she scanned the floor at the back of the emergency waiting room, he wasn't there. Not on the floor, reading KC's story, as he had been earlier. Nor had he moved to the waiting room seats.

Jamie tore across to the exit that opened onto short-term parking. She pulled open the door, and as if on cue, Wes walked in, her notebook under his arm. He took one look at her face and pulled her to him.

"What happened? Did your patient die?"

"*Casey* died."

Wes frowned. "Casey is a ghost. Therefore …"

"No. He was alive and in our coma ward."

"Good lord." Wes felt fortunate to have read widely in speculative fiction. Not so speculative today, was it? "So, his body was here the whole time, but somehow his spirit, his consciousness—or his unconsciousness—found you?"

Jamie nodded. Tears welled and poured down her cheeks, into her mouth, down her neck, and inside her collar.

A fellow sitting nearby, as kind as he was curious, offered them a little packet of tissues. Wes thanked him and handed them to Jamie to dry her face. She could see that he wanted to ask questions, but her tears, it seemed, were preventing him. She scrubbed her face with the tissues and made herself stop crying.

"Please just say what you want to," she told him. "I'm okay. And we have a little time. Before the van comes back."

Wes looked closely at her and nodded. "Then, forgive me for asking, but how did we not think that KC might be a twenty-year-old coma victim in your ward? Wouldn't that be obvious?"

Jamie almost laughed. "He wasn't twenty. He hadn't been twenty since 1937."

"I see. No, I don't. But I might, when I've thought about that for a while. I can think while I drive, which I should do before that van gets back. If you still think we should."

Jamie took her notebook from him. "I do. I really do, but first I need to see if KC has anything more to say."

"You just said he's dead. We can't bring him back to life. But we can get you out of here before those two come back in their van looking for you. Whoever they are. Churleys or registrars, bad guys or government employees."

"Just give me a few minutes to make sure there's no more writing. Then I'd like a ride to get my escape bag and go to the bus station."

"To go where?"

"Wherever the bus goes." She squeezed her eyes shut and held her pen over an empty page in her notebook. "Come on, KC. You must have something to say."

Wes peered out of the emergency room doors. "How many times have you left your job and apartment to run for it?"

"This will be three."

"Jamie, for my sake, could you for now keep it in the conditional? *If you run, then it will be three.*"

"I could keep it entirely hypothetical, for what it's worth. *If* I decided to run, this *would be* my third successful escape."

"I like the hypothetical, thanks."

"Wes, I can't joke. There isn't time. Come *on*, KC."

"Look, let's talk about your options." He put his arm around her. "It's rush hour. Even if they've searched the whole hospital on the far side of town, they're stuck in traffic on the bridge. We have time to decide what to do."

"I can only see one thing to do."

"Those two were scary, all right, but if they're Churleys, would they hit you over the head and carry you off? I can't see it happening, even if I weren't here."

Of course they would, but only as a last resort, for that was not how they preferred to operate. "The Churleys don't look frightening. They can even appear to be friendly when they want to, which is why I was happy to let them adopt me when I was a kid. It's a big part of why they're good at what they do."

"Do they have guns?"

"They own guns. I've never known them to use them."

"How would they force you to come back, then?"

"It's useless to talk about this."

"Jamie, I'm sorry, but I'm new to the situation. I need less ifs and thens, and more facts."

Jamie gazed down at the notebook on her lap. She didn't want to tell him the facts, because they were shameful.

Wes covered his face with his hands. "Okay. Let me think. We can't rush into some dead end."

"You keep saying *we*. I've only known you ten days."

Wes blinked. Jamie felt her cheeks grow hot.

She said, "Sorry. You're great. And here it is: the Churleys have the power to take me back with them without guns or even violence, because I'm like them."

"You're nothing like those two. They're criminals."

Jamie took a deep breath. "So am I."

"That's not even a hypothetical," Wes said. "You were coerced, confined, and forced to marry. How are you a criminal?"

"I made the fraudster calls."

That was what she hated most to remember. Not being locked up in darkness, not being kept alone in her room, and then in her shared room with Kam. Not missing a life of friends, travel, co-workers, and vacations. What she was ashamed to remember was the sound of the voices on the other end of the phone. Listening, trusting, and hoping. While she gently talked them out of their savings.

Her victims' wish to better themselves made them vulnerable. Their age and circumstances made them victims, just as she and her mother in the rice fields of Vietnam, with guns at their backs, were victims. *Either this or not, daughter. See what comes.* The hard truth was, she deserved jail.

She said, "I worked for Mags and Daino. Since I married Kam, I'm a member of their family. One of their gang. So is Kam. I don't want to go to jail, and above all I don't want Kam to spend his last days of life under police investigation. I love him, and I want him to have all the time he can with Brad. So I can't even turn myself in."

"But you want to visit him, and you think you won't get caught."

"I want to visit him, and I might get caught. Even if I don't, I'll have to run to stay out of jail and away from the Churleys."

She set pen and notebook on her lap, reached for his hand, and held it tight. "So even if you were to come with me, it would only be to hide. That's no kind of a life."

"I'd be happy in a cupboard with you."

Jamie smiled. "If there were books in the cupboard."

"Granted. But I mean it."

"Thanks. I feel like that too. Except I've been in a cupboard, when I was with the Churleys, and I don't want that for you."

"If we were on the run, though? Like *The Fugitive?* It could be an interesting kind of life."

Jamie thought of Casey, and the life he had longed for when he was twenty. Always moving, striding from adventure to adventure, gathering no moss. No children, no partner, no pet, no home. In the end he'd chosen a life of safety and excellent company. He'd chosen work that gave him time with his Carol, Pete, and Dylan. And even though he'd had his regrets, she was very damn sure that if offered the chance, he'd have chosen Carol, Pete, and Dylan again.

"It's not as interesting as it looks, when you're forced to live on the run. You'd hate it in the end. You might even hate me."

Wes sent her a sideways look. "Unlikely."

"Then I'd hate me. Because, Wes, your family is great. Gloria and your sisters, all your writing friends. That's what I want for you. Adventures, sure, but always your phenomenal family and friends to come back to."

Wes scowled. "I want that for you too, since you like my troublemaking family so much."

Jamie grimaced. "Maybe the police will catch all of us Churleys, and that will take the perilous choices away from me. I'll go to jail. You can bring me bread and cheese."

"And paperback novels?" Wes considered. "No, there's got to be a better way to get free of this situation."

"I've never found one."

"You've never, but *we* will. Let's think on it. Something you said twigged an idea."

Jamie looked out the door. "You still have a few minutes to think."

"And you have time to say your goodbyes to everybody here, if you're really going to go."

"I can't say them. I never say them. I just go."

"Then don't say goodbye. But say something, so that if you do vanish, they'll remember the last nice thing you said."

"And if I get thrown in jail, they'll have a good quote for the newspapers."

"Enough joking." Wes let out a long breath. "Go. Have a last word with your friends, and come back. I'll try to have an idea."

Jamie blinked. "I just had one."

"Okay."

"The quickest way for me to see Kam is to go see if that's Mags and Daino in the van, and, if it is, to ask them to take me there."

"You'd better be joking."

Jamie shot him a look. She was perfectly serious. If it was them, and at heart she was almost certain it was, they'd found her so quickly this time that it was inevitable they'd take her someday soon. "Keep your eyes open for trouble."

"Teach your grandmother," Wes answered lightly. "I'm a big reader, and there's nothing I don't know about antagonists." He squeezed her arm and took up his observation post at the emergency room door.

CHAPTER 15

Once Jamie was out of his sight, Wes moved closer to the window overlooking the Emergency parking lot to watch for the van's return. If these were the Churleys, a possibility that seemed more likely the less he wished it to be true, it was vital that he think of some ruse to send them on their way. Permanently. If he failed in this, he had a dreadful hunch that

Jamie, like a fox weary of the hunt, or a fox longing to see her beloved and dying Kam, would run to them and let them drive her off in their damned blue van.

He took his paperback copy of *The Last Gentleman* out of his pocket but put it back again. Walker Percy was matchless, but this was no time for southern courtesy or literary family drama. What was needed here in this crowded emergency room with doors that opened to the visitor's parking lot, was once again that superbly written and well-muscled John D MacDonald action hero, Travis McGee. There were twenty-one novels in the series, and each one presented an education in handling the life-or-death moments that for most people arrive seldom but swiftly, and without nearly enough warning. For years Wes had ordered the family shop's selection of novels for the wire rack, and he read them all before they were sent to the rack. Handled them gently, of course, so as not to crease the spines. He tried to recall some of McGee's clever and muscular moves, but the remembered cover of *The Long Blue Goodbye* got in the way. *The Long Blue Goodbye* referred to the look in a dead woman's eye, and it reminded Wes that even McGee couldn't save everyone.

But Wes could save one person. He could hustle Jamie out from under the Churleys' noses and keep her out of jail as well. He'd have to enter her world to do it, stand by her when she turned in the Churleys and herself at the police station, and wait for her for hours on hard benches outside — and inside — courtrooms. Her world of oaths and criminal revelations was an unlikely match for his own, rich in family and friendships. He'd had the benefit of living in a world where the corner store supported him and his, and where a colony of poets, journalists, and fiction writers stood ready to welcome him. A few more writers to study, and he would be able to stake his own claim to authorship and make a serious stab at a writing life.

It occurred to him that a writing life had been Casey's goal as well. A different writing life, of course; Casey's goals for his career had been far more adventurous. Personally, Wes would rather stack up pages of a manuscript any day than risk a spy's bullet or climb the Himalayas to write a story. But even his own quiet, enduring ambition would have to go on hold. He reckoned that if he and Jamie somehow managed a safe farewell visit with Kam in hospital, Jamie would, after his death, insist on going to the police. He was certain that not even Batman, Travis McGee, and the Last Gentleman together would be able to talk her out of it. Then the Churleys would go to jail, which was an excellent place for them; but so would Jamie, even with some kind of a deal.

He couldn't force her to let the Churleys sustain their criminal enterprise in order to keep her freedom. Furthermore, he didn't want to, when he considered all the elderly victims the Churleys were sucking the life savings from with their blandishing voices.

Nonetheless, he had to find some way to keep Jamie out of prison. He must know somebody who could see the coercion behind the criminality and do something about it. How stupid that he numbered no acquaintances among policemen or local politicians. He only knew writers and regular customers of the corner store.

Once again, the feeling that he was overlooking something important tugged at him. He got to his feet and told himself not to think about it. For now, he must remain vigilant for the return of the Churleys' blue van.

Inspiration would surely come when he was looking elsewhere.

Chapter 16

In Jamie's experience, it took most families between twenty minutes and half an hour to leave the room once the time of death had been called. So it was that instead of greeting her co-workers one last time, she came face to face with Carol and Pete Cooper, followed by a slump-shouldered Dylan, outside room 37. They closed the door on Kitchener Cooper's room. Dylan's grandmother looked as pale as the walls around her.

Jamie said, "I'm so sorry."

Carol answered, "Thanks, Jamie. It's Jamie, right? For taking care of my Kitchener."

"My pleasure, truly. He was something, wasn't he?"

The old lady nodded. She took her son's arm and walked away past her grandson, who was slouching against the wall not far from room 37. His dad called to him to follow.

Jamie glanced at Dylan. Should she speak to him? He only knew her as an orderly. A stranger. And nothing she could say would help him now.

But Dylan pushed himself away from the wall and walked straight up to her, determination clear on his face. How odd, that Jamie knew so much about this kid, and he knew nothing about her. It was like looking out through the dark side of a mirror.

Dylan asked, "Do you need a ride or anything?"

"I've got one, but thanks for the offer, Dylan."

"Okay. Thanks, for my grandfather, taking care of him and all that."

She wished she could tell him everything. But she only said, "You're welcome, of course. I liked him."

"You should have known him." Dylan bit his lip. "There was nobody——"

He bit off the end of the sentence, turned, and walked away from her.

Jamie called him back. He swivelled with an awkward step around an orderly's mop to retrace his path.

Jamie said, "In the children's ward, lots of them are stuck in bed with nothing to do. Got any ideas?"

He stared at her.

Choosing her words with care, Jamie said, "I'm thinking of the agreement between you and a certain insurance salesman of our mutual acquaintance."

Dylan shoved his hands in his pockets. Jamie knew any decision he might make would not be easy, and she thought that was probably the point.

Finally, he said, "How about a thirty-inch TV screen and a state-of-the-art computer games system with seventeen game cartridges?"

"Drop it off any time tomorrow. Well done. You'll miss them, though."

Dylan drew a line on the damp linoleum floor with the toe of his shoe. "I'm going to be too busy to play anymore, anyway. You know? I've got things to do in my life."

"Have adventures? Go places?"

"Exactly." He shoved his fists deep into his trouser pockets and was halfway down the corridor when he stopped short and threw his arms wide. A trolley swerved around him, and the orderly stared.

Dylan spoke in a clear young voice to the ceiling. "You hear that, KC? I kept my part of the agreement. I'll do things with my life and make my mark."

He paused, as if listening.

Louder, he called out, "KC, are you still here? Did you keep your side of the bargain?"

Nobody answered.

With a sudden burst of speed, Dylan tore away down the corridor after his family. Jamie almost laughed aloud. She guessed she had a few doors to step through, too. What a stupid idea it had been to give herself up to the Churleys. That was indeed the easy path. A path leading backwards. Not just a return, but a devolution, now that she'd had a taste of life with the Gates family.

I will if you will, she silently told KC.

She turned and, with a start, found beautiful Zane at her shoulder, staring after Dylan.

"Mars bars with nuts, that kid."

"Not so bad, actually," Jamie said.

"Do you want a ride home now your shift's up? The urologist I've been wanting you to meet is heading out pretty soon."

"I've got a ride, thanks," Jamie said.

She looked past Zane. Wes was walking along the corridor towards them.

Zane raised perfect brows and walked off, talking over her shoulder. "Oh my, you certainly do."

Jamie took Wes's hand.

"Time to make tracks?"

"Yes. And I want to tell you my idea for dealing with your criminal situation," he said. "I told you there was something I almost thought of. Now I thought of it."

"Tell me. But not here. Is it safe to go out to the car?"

"I think so, but I'll double-check using my now-practised oblique shadow-sheltered private detective surveillance technique."

He peered through the glass doors to Emergency and pronounced the parking lot safe for evasive movement. Hand in hand, they ran for his LeMans. As they drove towards the exit, a blue van pulled by them into the entry lane. Jamie saw Mags and Daino in the big front window, both of them looking towards the Emergency entrance.

"It's them," she said.

"And here we are, turning right out of the parking lot and getting clean away." Wes squeezed Jamie's hand. "What if we go to your place? You get your travel bag, while I make a quick call to Kam's hospital. If he's able to have visitors …"

"If he's alive," Jamie said heavily. They were nearing her apartment, and she was about to cut connections with everything she valued. Her job, her patients, her co-workers, the Gateses, and most of all Wes.

He said, "Then, we drive across country together in the good old LeMans, while the Churleys are still looking for you here. You go into the hospital to visit Kam."

Jamie shot him a grateful look. "It's three thousand miles."

Wes patted the dash. "This beauty can do it."

"Then, after I see Kam, I go to the police."

"Well, here's where it gets really interesting. I said I had an idea. I know a guy."

"A lawyer?" Jamie frowned. "A lawyer who works for free?"

"Well …"

"Who, then?"

"A poet."

Jamie did her best to hide her disappointment. Unless … "I guess a poet could also be an undercover detective?"

"Not this one. You remember him, I think. He gave a reading

at our place."

"The marsupial poet?"

"The other one, who writes about rotting fish and hands cut off."

"Okay." Jamie forced herself to keep her tone polite. They were almost at her apartment, and so far Wes's plan for the immediate future seemed to show a weak grasp of criminal situations.

"Well, poetry pays poorly, so he also writes for the daily city paper."

"That's news to me," Jamie said.

"It's news to everybody." He caught her look. "I mean, he writes the news. Get this, now. You tell him your story, and he agrees to write it."

"What if he doesn't?"

"One word. Gloria."

They nodded. No further explanation was required.

Jamie's heart lightened. "And then we go to the police."

"And they raid the Churleys and put them on trial and in jail."

"And me."

"Maybe." Wes frowned. "But there's such a thing as immunity for testimony, backed up by the newspaper article. And if not, they're bound to keep the sentence light for a coerced minor, which you were, and ..."

"... you'll bring me bread and cheese."

"Not just that. I'll pick you up outside the prison when you're released."

If she did go to jail, and there was a good chance she would, she deserved it. "If I don't go to jail, I can stop running. At least until the Churleys are released."

"You can change your name," Wes said. "Again, I mean."

"To what?"

"To mine. Don't laugh."

The proposal was so sudden, and so badly timed, that Jamie did just that. She apologized. "I'm not laughing at you. I'm laughing because of a release of tension."

"Sure." Wes's good nature remained apparently unruffled. "A natural reaction in a difficult time. I'd just like to say, though, no wonder Travis McGee never gets permanently involved with women."

Wes pulled up in front of her building. They agreed that Jamie would collect her bag from her bedroom closet and add to its contents as she saw fit, while he made the call to Kam's hospital. He was saying goodbye and thanks into the phone when she returned with the bag and a few more treasures she would have regretted leaving behind, including a photo of the Orzalina sisters and their pups, the Walker Percy novel *Love in the Ruins* that she'd borrowed from Wes, and the many pages of KC Cooper's ghost writing. If she could still call it that.

Wes hung up and turned to her. The look on his face told her the news was bad. As grievous, in fact, as it could be.

"I can't believe we missed him by an hour. Switchboard didn't know, and they put me through to the room. I talked to Brad. It was peaceful, and Kam's gone. I'm so sorry, Jamie."

Jamie leaned against her kitchen counter. She tried to take in the fact of two deaths in the same hour. Casey and Kam. It ought to help that those whom both men loved best had been with them at the last. Just as she'd been there when her mother died. None of them had been alone. That was something.

Nor was Jamie alone. She walked into Wes's arms. They would

drive off under the stars in Wes's LeMans until morning, and then take an early breakfast to the Gateses' house to share with Gloria and the girls. Jamie would talk to the poet who was really a newspaper reporter — or the newspaper reporter who was really a poet. And then to the police. She might or might not go to jail. Either way, she would put the stack of papers that was KC Cooper's story away in a box. Perhaps they would give it to Dylan someday.

Alternatively, perhaps they would just let things be.

Either this or not, daughter. See what comes of each.

Her mother was right. She would choose, and if she chose wrongly, she'd correct her mistake. And then, sooner or later, she and Wes would get on with their own good lives.

But that was not, as it turned out, the end of it. Two things, of a more ghostly nature, were still to happen that night.

First, there was the behaviour of the door to room 37, the room which a comatose KC Cooper had occupied all those weeks. About the time Jamie and Wes left her apartment, not very long after Dylan had declared his life intentions to the corridor ceiling, a small but important action occurred which nobody up or down the corridor witnessed.

Slowly, smoothly, room 37's door opened. All on its own.

The second event took place sometime later that night, inside Jamie's straw bag as it lay beside her feet under the dashboard of Wes's LeMans. Neither she nor Wes noticed the event at the time, because they were driving through the quiet town, heading towards the countryside and open sky for a few hours before the world woke up. Later, when Jamie found evidence of this latest manifestation, she decided that KC was, after all, too polite to take her hand in his when she had pointedly asked him not to.

Instead, the pen had moved by itself inside her straw bag, and written on the open lines towards the bottom of the last page.

KC's round handwriting looked more hurried than ever. The words rambled on the page, stopped and started, and ended in jagged trailing tails. It seemed, now that KC really was a ghost, he had time to scrawl only a few words.

I pull, Jamie's pen wrote, with Jamie unaware.

I pull the door

The light

There was a scratchy line and then the writing began again.

Voices

Ted

What do you know

Ted

I step through the door, KC wrote.

Wes and Jamie drove away through the night.

Beautiful

Later, they walked a while under the stars.

THE ARTISTS

Herman Lau
Cover artist, Solstice Ritual
Herman Lau is a freelance artist from Edmonton, Alberta. His interests in illustration stem from the stories and games he grew up with, mythologies full of movement and characters to inspire his drawn illusions. His artwork has been published locally and internationally, including at an exhibition at the Museum of American Illustration in New York and in a collection at State Library Victoria, Australia. He has also run children's visual art programs for non-profit organizations and galleries and provided graphic facilitation services for various municipal groups and initiatives. Find more of Herman's work at paintedmonk.wordpress.com, and on Instagram @paintedmonk.

This is Herman's third *Pulp Literature* cover, the first being *Purple Siren* for Issue 22, Spring 2019, and *Black Tortoise Kowtows* for Issue 34, Spring 2022. About *Solstice Ritual*, Herman says, "The tiger inked on her sternum begins to hiss, and she knows she is not alone."

Rina Piccolo
Creator, 'Say Cheese, Jesus, Please'
Spanning a decades-long career in comics, Rina Piccolo's work has been seen in *The New Yorker, Barron's Business Magazine, Reader's Digest,* and more. She has been syndicated with King Features Syndicate since 2000 with three comic features: *Six*

Chix (2000–2016), *Tina's Groove* (2002–2017), and currently *Rhymes With Orange* (2017–present). Rina co-authored and illustrated the book *Quirky Quarks: A Cartoon Guide to the Fascinating Realm of Physics* (Springer Publishing, 2016). She is also the creator of 'The Comic of The Future' a digitally interactive cartoon titled 'The Gallery' (Mental Canvas, 2019/20.) Presently, she is working on a collection of comic short stories. When she's not making comics or scribbling in her art journal, Rina likes riding her bike, reading, and hanging out with friends and family. She lives in Toronto, and you can find her newsletter at rinapiccolo.substack.com.

'Say Cheese, Jesus, Please' is Rina's fourth work in *Pulp Literature*. Her illustrated story 'The Power of Centipedes' appeared in Issue 7 (Summer 2015), and was followed by 'The Vanishing Dot' in Issue 16 (Autumn 2017), and 'When a Double Flush Is Necessary' in Issue 26 (Spring 2020). We're delighted to have her back for this cheeky pen and ink wash one-pager, about which she says, "I grew up in an Italian-Canadian Catholic home, and so there is a lot of truth in this narrative. As a child I was afraid of almost everything, and I thank the universe that I can now look back on it all with an ink pen and a good dose of humour."

MEL ANASTASIOU
In-house illustrator
Mel Anastasiou loves drawing for *Pulp Literature* because she loves the stories she illustrates. She draws in black and white, working from imagination and inspired by details from Renaissance compositions. You can find illustrations, writing tips, and news about her books and novellas at melanastasiou.wordpress.com, and see more of her artwork on Facebook at Bird and Branch Artwork.

HALL OF FAME

These are the heroes — the Patrons and Pulp Literati whose monthly support helped bring you this issue. Please lift your glasses and give them a rousing cheer!

The Brewers
Dana Tye Rally

The Innkeepers
Abigail Bruce
Andrea Kepple
David Jensen
Ev Bishop
Gilles Cyrenne
Gillian Gardiner
Kevin Harris
Lorna Ens
Mark Francis
Richard Ohnemus
Robin McGillveray
Susan Jackson
Kevin S Moul

The Cicerones
Jennifer Sommersby
Roger & Anne Anastasiou
Zoë Ricard

The Bartenders
Alana Krider
Andrea Kirkham
Anna Belkine
Bjarne Hansen

Brighton Hugg
Bryan Moose
Chris Olee
Dave Wayne
Deepthi Atukorala
Devan Erno
Ernst Pulido
Evelyn Ann
Finnian Burnett
Hannah Moor
James Carlino
Jennifer Getsinger
Jillian Shoichet
Kat Hankinson
Katherine Derbyshire
kc dyer
Kelsey Brennan
Kim Seary
KT Wagner
Leny Wagner
Lin & John Richardson
Margot Landels
Margot Spronk
Megan Shaw
Michelle Balfour
Mike Sylvester
Peter Halasz
Rapscallion

Richard Gropp
Ron Graves
Scott F Gray
Shannon Saunders
Star
Suzanne Philip
Venasa Simpson

The Regulars
Adam Fout
Andy W
BC
Catherine Levinson
Charity Tahmaseb
Emmy Bee
James Gotaas
Jenny Blackford
JS Andrew
Marilyn Holt
Marta Salek
Meredith Frazier
Michelle Robinson
Paul Anguiano
Rina Piccolo
Sonia Brock
Vera

If you would like to join the ranks of these worthies, you can become a patron on Patreon at patreon.com/pulplit or join the Pulp Literati through our website at pulpliterature.com/join-pulp-literati/

In Memoriam

It is with great sadness we bid farewell to **John Fraser Richardson**, *who has been a loyal supporter of* Pulp Literature *since its inception. John passed away peacefully in November, surrounded by the love of his family. Please join us in lifting a glass of your tipple of choice in his memory.*

OUR SPONSORS

These generous individuals and companies contributed to our 2024 Keep the Presses Rolling fundraiser—which is why you can see this issue in print. Thank you so much!

Gold Level
Finnian Burnett
Amanda Bidnall Editorial
Academie Cavallo

Silver Level
Kate Heartfield
Surrey International
  Writers' Conference
Federation of BC Writers
Academie Duello
Danceability Studios
Renée Sarojini Saklikar

Bronze Level
Krista Wallace

General Level
JJ Lee
Jude Neale
Dale Adams Segal
Daniela Elza

Thank you to all of our donors, and to everyone who participated in the Silent Auction!

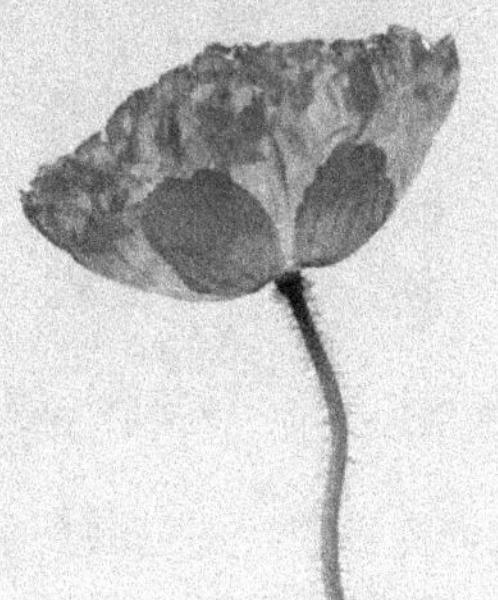

Commit these deadlines to memory

May 1, 2025
Far Horizons Award for Short Fiction | $1250
One winner gets the prize

August 1, 2025
Constance Rooke Creative
Nonfiction Prize | $1250
One winner takes all

November 1, 2025
Open Season Awards | $6000
Three writers split the winnings

malahatreview.ca
malahat@uvic.ca

ARC POETRY

The place to find great poetry!

Established in 1978, **ARC POETRY MAGAZINE** has been known as the premier poetry-focused journal in Canada for over 45 years. Each new issue contains exceptional essays on poetry, reviews of new Canadian poetry books, breath-taking visual art, and lots of new poetry by contemporary writers in Canada and from around the world.

Buy a copy of **ARC POETRY MAGAZINE** at your local magazine store, or order directly from us at arcpoetry.ca. You can also subscribe online or by mailing a cheque or money order to:
Arc, PO Box 81060, Ottawa, ON, K1P 1B1

$40 CAD for one year
$65 CAD for two years*

If you're looking for great Canadian poetry, look no further than ARC **POETRY**!

Prices listed for Canadian subscriptions
Visual art: Shalone Franklin, photographed
by Chris Brown

THE DREAMS ISSUE

Dreams are like short, strange films that our mind produces while we sleep. They take place in the theatre of the subconscious, that amorphous space that can seem familiar and unfamiliar at the same moment. A place where you wander, like a character in a shadowy noir mystery, trying to figure out what is going on, trying to make sense of a world that makes no sense … as if there is always an "explanation" for what is going on.

We invite you to mine the depths of your mind and send us your surrealist trips through dreamland — your beautiful nightmares, your daydreams, or dreams of the future.

"The dream is the small hidden door in the deepest and most intimate sanctum of the soul."
— Carl Jung

"We are like the dreamer who dreams and then lives inside the dream."
— The Upanishads

Forthcoming summer/fall 2025: submissions open January 2025.
subterrain.ca

Get on board with **Bookworm** for your *free* weekly dose of exclusive reviews, book excerpts, and much more.

Visit *reviewcanada.ca/TTC* or scan the code to the right.

Literary Review of Canada

A JOURNAL OF IDEAS

IGNITE YOUR IMAGINATION

30 yrs of award-winning sci-fi and fantasy

WWW.ONSPEC.CA

MARKETPLACE

$\mathcal{B}$OOKS

Advent *by Michael Kamakana* • We thought we knew what the aliens wanted. Think again. • pulpliterature.com/advent

Allaigna's Song: Chorale *by JM Landels* • The long-awaited conclusion to the bestselling *Allaigna's Song* trilogy. • pulpliterature.com/allaignas-song

The Extra: A Monument Studios Mystery *by Mel Anastasiou* • Extra Frankie Ray gets her big break on the Silver Screen, until murder steals the scene. • pulpliterature. com/the-extra

The Labours of Mrs Stella Ryman: Further Fairmount Mysteries *by Mel Anastasiou* • Trapped in a down-at-the-heels care home. You'd be cranky too. • pulpliterature.com/stella-ryman-and-the-fairmount-manor-mysteries

What the Wind Brings *by Matthew Hughes* • Winner of the 2020 Endeavour Award • pulpliterature.com/product-category/novels/matthew-hughes

The Writer's Boon Companion *by Mel Anastasiou* • Thirty Days Towards an Extraordinary Volume • pulpliterature.com/subscribe/the-bookstore

$\mathcal{B}$OOKSTORES

Russell Books • 100-747 Fort St, Victoria, BC • russellbooks.com

Western Sky Books • 2132-2850 Shaughnessy St, Port Coquitlam, BC V3C 6K5 • 604-461-5602•store.westernskybooks.com

White Dwarf / Dead Write Books • 3715 10th Ave W, Vancouver, BC V6R 2G5 • 604-228-8223 • whitedwarf@deadwrite.com

$\mathcal{C}$ONFERENCES & EVENTS

Surrey International Writers' Conference 24-27 October 2024 • siwc.ca

When Words Collide • August 2025 Calgary, AB • whenwordscollide.org

Wine Country Writers' Festival • Sep 2025 winecountrywriters-festival.ca

$\mathcal{P}$RINTING & PUBLISHING

First Choice Books/Victoria Bindery Book printing & binding • graphic design • eBooks • marketing materials 1-800-957-0561 • firstchoicebooks.ca

$\mathcal{W}$RITING RESOURCES

Dreamers Creative Writing • Workshops, residencies, contests & more! • www.dreamerswriting.com

Federation of BC Writers • Workshops • contests • networking & more! www.bcwriters.ca/join-us

MAGAZINES

Amazing Stories · Back in print! amazingstories.com

Arc Poetry Magazine · Poetry, essays, interviews, reviews · arcpoetry.ca

The Digest Enthusiast · Digests past & present plus new genre fiction larquepress.com

EVENT Magazine · Poetry & prose eventmagazine.ca

Geist · Ideas + Culture · Made in Canada · geist.com

Malahat Review · Poetry, fiction, creative non-fiction · www.malahatreview.ca

Mystery Weekly Magazine · The cutting edge of short mystery fiction www.mysteryweekly.com

Neo-opsis · Canadian magazine of science fiction based in Victoria, BC · neo-opsis.ca

OnSpec · The Canadian magazine of the fantastic · onspecmag.wordpress.com

Polar Borealis · Paying market for new Canadian SF&F writers & artists · polarborealis.ca

Room Magazine · Literature, Art & Feminism since 1975 · roommagazine.com

CONTESTS

Pulp Literature runs six annual contests for poetry, flash fiction, short stories, and novel first pages. For contest guidelines, prizes, and entry fees, see pulpliterature.com/contests.

The Bumblebee Flash Fiction Contest
Contest opens: 1 January 2025
Deadline: 15 February 2025
Winner notified: 15 March 2025
Winner published: Issue 47, Summer 2025
Prize: $300

The Magpie Award for Poetry
Contest opens: 1 March 2025
Deadline: 15 April 2025
Winner notified: 15 May 2025
Winner published: Issue 48, Autumn 2025
Prize: $500

The Hummingbird Flash Fiction Prize
Contest opens: 1 May 2025
Deadline: 15 June 2025
Winner notified: 15 July 2025
Winner published: Issue 49, Winter 2026
Prize: $300

The First Page Cage

Contest opens: 1 August 2025
Deadline: 15 September 2025
Winner notified: 15 October 2025
Quarter-finalists published online: Autumn 2025
Prize: $300

The Raven Short Story Contest

Contest opens: 1 September 2025
Deadline: 15 October 2025
Winner notified: 15 November 2025
Winner published: Issue 50, Spring 2026
Prize: $300

The Kingfisher Poetry Prize

Contest opens: 1 October 2025
Deadline: 15 November 2025
Winner notified: 15 December 2025
Winner published: Issue 50, Spring 2026
Prize: $300

PULP
Literature

The Bumblebee
Flash Fiction Contest
Deadline: 15 February
Prize $300

The Magpie Award for Poetry
Deadline: 15 April
Prize $500

The Hummingbird Flash Fiction Prize
Deadline: 15 June
Prize $300

The Raven Short Story Contest
Deadline: 15 October
Prize $300

The Kingfisher Poetry Prize
Deadline: 15 November
Prize $300

Enter today:
pulpliterature.com/contests

Allaigna's Song
Overture
JM Landels

PULP
Literature
JJ Lee
'The Man In the
Long Black Coat'

PULP
Literature
Carol Berg
Uncanonical Murder

PULP
Literature
Matthew Hughes
'The Devil You Don't'
Allaigna's Song: Aria

PULP
Literature
George McWhirter
Stalk

PULP
Literature

FANTASTIC
FRESH
FICTION

www.pulpliterature.com

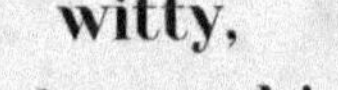

$\mathcal{B}$ECOME A PATRON OF PULP LITERATURE

By supporting *Pulp Literature* on Patreon with $2 or more per month, you will be laying the foundation for a secure future for the magazine, as well as ensuring that you never miss an issue! Your subscription includes four big issues of short stories, novellas, poetry, comics, and novel excerpts, delivered to your door or electronic mailbox each year. **Find us at patreon.com/pulplit**

If you prefer to subscribe through our website, go to pulpliterature. com/subscribe.

Or you can send a cheque with the form below to
Subscriptions, Pulp Literature Press, 21955 16 Ave, Langley BC, V2Z 1K5, Canada

- ❏ **Send me 2 years (8 issues) at the special rate of $110** (save $34)*
- ❏ **Send me 1 year (4 issues) for $60** (save $12)*
- ❏ **Send me 2 years of digital issues for $35** (save $12.92)
- ❏ **Send me 1 year of digital issues for $20** (save $3.96)

Name: ____

Address: ____

City: _________________________________ Prov. / State: _________

Postal code: _______________ Country:______________________

Email: ____

- ❏ Payment enclosed
- ❏ Bill me
- ❏ New
- ❏ Renewal

Make cheques payable in Canadian funds to Pulp Literature Press. Include email address for digital editions and Paypal billing, or subscribe at www.pulpliterature.com/subscribe.

*for postage outside Canada add $20 per year in North America or $32 per year overseas.

9 781988 865690